STINETINGLERS

All New Stories
by the
Master of
Scary Tales

STINETINGLERS

All New Stories
by the
Master of
Scary Tales

R.L. STINE

FEIWEL AND FRIENDS
NEW YORK

A Feiwel and Friends Book

An imprint of Macmillan Publishing Group, LLC

120 Broadway, New York, NY 10271 • mackids.com

Our books may be purchased in bulk for promotional, educational,
or business use. Please contact your local bookseller or the Macmillan
Corporate and Premium Sales Department at (800) 221–7945 ext.
5442 or by email at MacmillanSpecialMarkets@macmillan.com.

Library of Congress Cataloging-in-Publication Data

Names: Stine, R. L., author.
Title: Stinetinglers : all new stories by the master of scary tales / R. L.
    Stine.
Description: First edition. | New York : Feiwel and Friends, 2022. |
    Summary: A collection of ten scary stories with brief introductions by
    the author.
Identifiers: LCCN 2022017583 | ISBN 978-1-250-83627-4 (hardcover)
Subjects: LCSH: Horror tales, American. | Children's stories, American. |
    CYAC: Horror stories. | Short stories. | LCGFT: Horror fiction. | Short
    stories.
Classification: LCC PZ7.S86037 Stm 2022 | DDC [Fic]—dc23
LC record available at https://lccn.loc.gov/2022017583

First edition, 2022
Book design by Trisha Previte
Feiwel and Friends logo designed by Filomena Tuosto
Printed in the United States of America by Lakeside Book Company

ISBN 978-1-250-83627-4 (hardcover)

10 9 8 7 6 5 4 3 2 1

To Dylan and Mia

CONTENTS

INTRODUCTION

READERS, BEWARE. I wrote these new stories to give you a chill.

You know. That tingle you get at the back of your neck when you begin to feel afraid. Your skin turns cold and the little hairs stand on end. Your heart pumps and your teeth begin to chatter.

That tingling feeling when . . .

You think someone evil is watching you . . .

You don't know where you are or how to find your way home . . .

The terrifying howls are coming from your basement . . .

You can't stop yourself from becoming a creature you don't recognize . . .

The darkness surrounds you and there's no way out . . .

We all enjoy a good scare when we know the story isn't true. The stories in this book couldn't happen to *you*—could they?

I wrote them to take you to a Stinetingling world just beyond the real world . . . a world of shadows and fright and startling twists and surprises.

I hope these stories bring you to a place where the cold *tingle* becomes a SCREAM!

—R. L. Stine

WELCOME TO THE IN-BETWEEN

Have you ever felt that time has stopped moving? A long, long day in school. And every time you look up at the clock, it seems it hasn't moved at all. There are still hours to go!

I remember the intense pain of Christmas Eve, waiting for morning, for it to be late enough to open presents. Checking the clock beside my bed again and again—and the clock had barely moved.

I've written lots of stories about going back in time. But this is the first story I ever wrote about being stuck in time.

"GABE, PROMISE YOU WON'T BE LATE," MY FRIEND CARVER SAID.
He slapped my hockey stick with his. We were shooting a puck back and forth on Willmore Pond. The pond was frozen hard, and the ice was slick and smooth. It was a cold December afternoon, and I shivered under three layers of sweaters and a parka.

"Promise," I said. I swung my stick hard and sent the puck sliding past him. Carver spun around to chase after it and nearly fell off his skates.

He's a better skater than I am. He's on the Blazers, our middle school hockey team.

I'm not on any team. I'm not really into sports. But Carver likes to go on the ice with me. I guess because it makes him feel like a superstar.

"You always promise, and you're always late," he said.

He circled the puck and sent it back to me. "You're late for everything, Gabe, and I get tired of waiting for you."

"I think I'm getting one of those smart watches for Christmas," I said. "That should help."

The puck slid into the snow at the edge of the pond, and we both went after it. My breath steamed in front of me. I was getting a real workout.

"Know what?" Carver said. "It's bad news having my birthday on the day before Christmas. No one ever remembers or makes a fuss." He tapped the puck back onto the ice.

"But you're having a party—" I started.

"Yeah. I can't believe my parents actually remembered I wanted a birthday party," Carver replied. "So it's special, see. Please don't come late."

I raised my gloved right hand. "I swear I'll be early. Trust me. If I'm late, I'll eat this puck."

Carver grinned. "I'm going to remember that. Do you want it with ketchup or mustard?"

At home, I found Mom and Dad in the den, watching a reality show on Netflix about an octopus. "I never knew an octopus could have a personality," Dad said.

"Maybe we need a small one for the aquarium," Mom said.

"I don't think there *are* any small ones," Dad said.

They were so into the octopus show they didn't even see me in the doorway. "Can I talk to you?" I said.

They both turned. "You should watch this, Gabe," Dad said. "You'd learn a lot about undersea life."

"I learn about undersea life on *SpongeBob*," I replied.

They both laughed. They think I'm a riot.

I stepped in front of the TV. "Listen, I need a present for Carver," I told them.

Mom squinted at me through her glasses. "A Christmas present?"

"No. A birthday present. His birthday party is tomorrow afternoon."

They both shook their heads and frowned at me. "Why did you wait till the last minute?" Dad asked.

"Why are you always late, Gabe?" Mom added. She glanced at the tall grandfather clock in the corner of the den. "It's after six. All the stores will be closed."

"Well, can we go right after breakfast tomorrow?" I asked. "I really need to get him something."

"No way. Who has a birthday on Christmas Eve?" Dad asked.

"It wasn't his choice," I said.

They both laughed at that, too.

4

"We can go shopping tomorrow morning," Mom said. "Do you know what you want to buy him?"

"Not really," I said. "Maybe a hockey jersey or something. He's really into hockey."

"That's a good idea," Mom said. "But you should have thought of it sooner so we wouldn't have to go shopping on the day before Christmas."

"You're right," I said. "I need to start planning in advance." I turned to leave the den. "You know what? I'm going up to my room to work on my book report right now, even though school is on winter break."

I climbed the stairs to my room. I didn't tell them that my book report was over a week late. I also hadn't finished reading the book. But I thought I could write the report anyway.

We have a long hall upstairs. There are four bedrooms up here. Mine is down at the end. I stopped halfway, in front of the guest room. The room was small with bright yellow wallpaper, a bed and a dresser, and one chair.

We were expecting my cousins from Michigan to come for Christmas. But my uncle got sick and they had to cancel. So, the guest room was empty.

But I had a good reason to stop there. The guest room closet was where my parents always hid my Christmas presents. Always the same closet. They didn't know that I knew.

Should I sneak in and take a peek? Why was I asking the question? It's what I do every year.

I turned toward the stairway and listened. My parents hadn't moved from the den and their octopus movie. I took a deep breath and plunged into the guest room.

The closet was long and narrow. A ceiling light flashed on when I slid open the door. The closet held some old winter coats and a pile of beat-up sneakers. I could see a bunch of wrapped presents down on the floor against the back wall.

Ducking under the coats, I dropped to my knees to examine the gifts. The first box I picked up was long and pretty heavy. Did they buy me a new PlayStation? I shook it. No. It felt like clothes.

I set it back down and picked up a few more boxes. I raised a thin rectangular box wrapped in silver paper. It was very light. Maybe Bluetooth earbuds?

It was getting warm in the closet. Or was it just me? I listened hard. I didn't hear anyone approaching. Working fast, I tore open the wrapping paper.

"Yes!" I whispered. "They bought it for me!"

A smart watch. I unfolded the wristband and studied it. *Awesome!*

This was the coolest! Now I could send texts and make calls and do all kinds of amazing things right on my watch.

I couldn't resist. I had to try it on. My hand was actually

shaking as I wrapped the red plastic band around my wrist and fastened it. I raised it to my face and read the dial: 6:10.

Now I'll never be late, I told myself. *Because I'm never taking this watch off.*

I gasped when I heard a soft *thud* and then a scraping sound. Footsteps? One of my parents was climbing the stairs.

I had to put the watch back in the wrapping paper and get out of the closet. But a wave of panic swept over me. I couldn't breathe. I tugged the watch off, tugged harder than I should have.

The watch slipped from my hand. Hit the hard closet floor. Bounced. And hit again.

I let out a cry as I heard a *crack*ing sound.

Oh no! The dial shattered. The battery flew out onto the floor.

I'm going to be caught! I thought, my heart suddenly pounding. *How can I ever explain?*

I grabbed the broken watch off the floor and jammed it into my jeans pocket. It took three tries to fumble my fingers around the tiny battery. I shoved it into my pocket, too.

I scrambled from the closet. Crept out into the hall. No one there. *Whew.* I ran back to my room and closed the door.

I dropped down in front of my laptop and tried to start my book report. I was writing about a book of Greek myths and legends. The stories were pretty awesome. I'd read almost half the book, enough to write a good report.

But my heart was still fluttering from my close call. And I couldn't concentrate. I kept thinking about the broken watch. How would I ever explain it to my parents?

I couldn't tell them the truth. That I've been sneaking looks at my Christmas presents since I was seven. But I couldn't think of a good explanation for how the watch got messed up.

Maybe if I wrapped it up again and put it back with the other presents? Then I could open it on Christmas morning and everyone would think the watch had arrived broken from the store?

It just might work. Or maybe not. I was so excited to see the watch, I tore the gift wrapping. I couldn't make it look like new if I tried.

Thinking about this terrible problem, I didn't get a single sentence of my book report written. And now, I was yawning and my eyelids felt heavy.

It must be late, I thought. I climbed up from my desk and walked downstairs to say good night.

I was surprised to find my parents still in the den. An octopus uncurled its tentacles on the TV screen. They turned as I stepped into the room.

I yawned. "I got a good start on my book report," I told them. "But I started to get tired. Just wanted to say good night."

They both blinked. Dad's mouth dropped open. "Gabe, since when do you go to bed before dinner?" he said.

"Dinner?" I turned my eyes to the grandfather clock against the wall. It read 6:10.

But how could that be?

"You have time to finish your report," Mom said. "I'm not going to start dinner until this octopus show is over. It should be around seven."

I yawned again. Something was weird here, but I was too sleepy to think about it clearly.

"If you're sleepy," Dad said, "go upstairs and take a nap. We'll wake you in time for dinner. It's your favorite tonight. My homemade pizza with hot dogs on it."

"Awesome," I said. On the TV, a man was feeding something to the octopus.

I climbed back upstairs and lay down on top of my bed. I fell asleep very quickly, a deep, dreamless sleep. I'm not sure how long I was out. When I woke up, the sky outside my window was still evening gray.

I felt rested. So I sat back down at my keyboard and

started to write the book report. I wrote quickly, my fingers tapping away. Writing is easy for me, I guess, because I enjoy it. I almost never have to struggle to write reports and essays.

I worked for maybe an hour. I kept stopping, listening for my parents to call me to dinner. I stood up when I realized my stomach was growling. I was seriously hungry.

I hurried down the stairs, taking them two at a time. My parents were still on the couch in the den. "Is it dinnertime?" I called from the doorway. "I'm starving!"

"Too early," Dad said. He kept his eyes on the underwater scene on the TV. "I'm going to put the pizza in the oven when this is over at seven."

"Huh? Seven?" I turned to the big clock in the corner of the den. It read 6:10.

No way.

"I think that clock stopped," I said.

"No, it didn't." Mom glanced at the phone she held in her lap. "The clock is right. It's six ten."

"Do you want to watch with us, Gabe?" Dad asked. "This is the best part. The octopus is starting to understand some words."

"Uh . . . no thanks," I said.

My brain was spinning. I hauled myself back up to my room, sat down on the edge of my bed, and texted Carver. *What time is it?*

My phone rang two seconds later. "Is that a joke?" Carver asked. "Why are you asking me what time it is?"

"Just answer the question," I said. "I think my phone is—"

"It's six ten," Carver said. "What time did you think it was?"

"Well, I have a little problem," I started. "You see—"

"I can't talk," Carver interrupted. "We're having supper. My parents are trying to grab my phone. I'm not allowed to use it at the table."

"Okay. Sorry," I said. "See you at your party tomorrow."

"Don't be late," Carver said. Then he clicked off.

"Late?" I said to myself. "How can I be on time if I never get past six ten at night?"

I tugged the smart watch from my pocket and sat down at my desk to study it. Did I somehow stop time when I accidentally smashed the watch? What a weird thought. Of course, something like that only happens in scary TV shows and movies.

I squinted at the watch in the bright light from my desk lamp. The screen had a jagged crack across it. It looked like a bolt of lightning. The time stood in orange numbers against a black background: 6:10.

I shook the watch. I raised it above my head and shook it some more.

The numbers didn't change. Under the cracked lens,

the watch still read 6:10. I tried pushing the tiny buttons on the side. Then I shook it some more.

6:10.

"This isn't happening," I told myself.

I had an idea. *I'll go to sleep. I'll sleep for hours. When I wake up, it will have to be later. It will be breakfast time, and everything will return to normal.*

I tucked the broken watch back into my jeans pocket. Then I pulled on my pajamas and tucked myself into bed.

I'm not sure how long I slept, but it had to be several hours. I dreamed that Carver and I were being chased down the street by an octopus. We tried to fight it off with hockey sticks. But the octopus just kept on coming.

The dream stayed in my mind as I made my way downstairs to breakfast.

A cold feeling of dread made me stop at the doorway to the den. Mom and Dad sat on the couch watching an octopus swirling around underwater.

"Time for breakfast?" I asked in a tiny voice.

They both turned toward me and laughed. "Are you being funny, Gabe? Why are you in your pajamas? We haven't had dinner yet. It's only ten after six."

"Are you totally confused?" Dad asked.

"Maybe," I replied. I squinted at them. "Didn't I come

down here a couple of times already and ask you what time it was?"

"No," Mom answered. "You didn't. Are you trying to play some kind of joke on us?"

"Why are you acting weird?" Dad demanded. "Just because Christmas is the day after tomorrow?"

I sighed. *Maybe Christmas will never come.*

I suddenly felt dizzy, kind of woozy, like an octopus was swimming in my brain. I made my way to the front closet and grabbed my down jacket. Then I crept out of the house, closing the door silently behind me.

I needed to think. I needed fresh air. A burst of cold air made me shiver. I zipped my jacket to the top. A pale full moon was rising in the gray sky.

I didn't pay any attention to where I was walking. Cars rumbled past. I saw some people just getting home from work in time for dinner. I passed the empty lot at the end of the block and kept walking.

I kept thinking that maybe, if I took a really long walk, the time would move again and it would be dinnertime when I returned home. The truth is, I didn't know what to think.

I started to run. Maybe I could outrun time.

I knew I wasn't thinking clearly. But how could I?

I found myself at the playground in front of the

elementary school. *How far did I run?* My heart was pounding and my legs throbbed.

Two large dogs were growling and grunting, having fun wrestling and jumping on each other near the soccer field. No one else around. I plopped down on a playground swing and waited to catch my breath.

I started to reach into my pocket for the watch—when everything went dark. I mean, it was like someone turned off all the lights. I gazed up at the sky, which was a solid black now. The pale full moon had vanished.

I blinked a few times, waiting for my eyes to adjust. After a few seconds the trees and houses across the street came into view, black against the charcoal sky.

It took me a while to realize I was no longer alone.

In the total darkness, something moved at the edge of the playground. I heard the shuffle of feet on the grass. Several kids came into view. They moved toward me silently.

I jumped up from the swing. "Hey—!"

Too dark. I couldn't see their faces.

No one spoke. I called out again. "Hey—!" I took a step toward them.

Moving quickly, they formed a circle around me. They pressed in on me, dark figures, solid black against the black sky. I squinted hard.

And then I let out a startled cry when I realized *they didn't have faces!*

They were shadows. Silent shadows in a tight circle around me.

No eyes. No faces. Kids made of shadow.

"I—I—" I stammered, unable to find words.

And then one of them finally spoke. "Welcome," a girl shadow said, her voice a soft whisper floating on the cold air. "Welcome to the In-Between."

I gasped. "Huh? What are you talking about? Who *are* you?"

"Welcome," a boy said in a hoarse whisper. "We came to welcome you."

"Welcome me to *what*?" My voice cracked. "Why can't I see you?"

"We are the kids of the In-Between," the girl said. "You are one of us now."

My brain was spinning. I was desperate to figure out what these kids wanted. "You're in some kind of club?" I said. "What's an In-Between club? What are you talking about?"

"We are caught between time," the girl said in her throaty whisper.

"We can't go forward or back," another boy said. "We are stuck, and now you are, too. Stuck in between time."

"You—you're trying to scare me," I stammered.

"No. We're here to *welcome* you," the girl said.

And then they all began to chant in a low whisper . . .

"Welcome to the In-Between . . .

"Welcome to the In-Between . . .

"Welcome to the In-Between . . ."

Their voices rumbled in my ears, growing louder as they repeated the words.

"Stop!" I shouted. "Stop it! Go away! Leave me alone!"

"Welcome to the In-Between . . .

"Welcome to the In-Between . . .

"Welcome to the In-Between . . ."

"Nooooo!" A terrified howl burst from my throat. I lurched forward. Tried to run.

But they pressed tightly around me, a shadowy wall. I couldn't break through. No way to escape.

"Welcome to the In-Between . . .

"Welcome to the In-Between . . ."

As I stared at them in horror, a girl reached out her shadowy hand and touched my shoulder.

"Ohh," I groaned as I felt the cold of her touch seep into my skin.

She grabbed my hand. Her fingers felt like icicles. I shuddered as the cold swept over my arm.

"Welcome to the In-Between . . .

"Welcome to the In-Between . . ."

A boy touched my forehead with his gray shadow hand. My skin froze under his touch.

My hand tingled, numb where the girl held it. She

finally let go, and I stared down at it. Gray now. Gray and numb. My hand was a shadow hand!

"Nooooo." I let out a howl.

I grabbed a boy's arm. I couldn't feel it. My hand slid right off.

I could hear my own breathing. I felt weak. I could feel myself slipping into the gray. Disappearing . . .

My arms . . . my legs . . . all darkening to shadows. I was becoming one of them!

"Welcome to the In-Between . . .

"Welcome to the In-Between . . ."

"Whooooaaaa!" Another cry escaped my throat, weaker this time, my voice mostly air.

Panic made my whole body tremble. I could feel the world going into shadow. Feel myself fading away.

"Welcome . . .

"Welcome . . ."

Their chant repeated in my ears. I couldn't move. I couldn't *think*.

I had to do something. I fumbled for the broken watch in my jeans pocket. I tugged it out. Then I dug into the pocket until I found the tiny battery.

I held the watch in one hand, the battery between the fingers of my other hand.

Both hands were trembling shadows. I couldn't feel them. I could barely see them.

I took a deep breath. I shut my eyes. And I jammed the battery into the back of the watch.

"Whoa!"

An explosion of sound made my ears ring. I fell to my knees. The sky rumbled and the ground beneath me shook. The roar of the explosion made my head feel like it was about to splatter apart.

When the sound finally faded, I opened my eyes. The chanting had stopped. The shadow kids were gone.

I raised my eyes to the sky. Evening gray again. The pale full moon was back, floating just above the trees.

Was time moving again?

I ran all the way home. Dad met me at the door. "Gabe, where did you go? We had to hold up dinner for you."

"You should have told us you were going out," Mom said. "It's after seven thirty."

"Yessss!" I cried. "Yesss!" I hugged them both. I wanted to cry. I wanted to jump up and down and cheer.

I pumped both fists in the air. "I'm back! I'm back! I'm not an In-Betweener!" I shouted.

"What are you talking about?" Mom demanded. "You're acting totally weird. Go wash your hands and sit down for dinner."

On my way to the bathroom, I walked past the den and

glanced at the tall grandfather clock: 7:35. "Yessss!" I ran up to the clock and kissed it. Then I hurried to get ready for dinner.

The next morning, Dad took me to an electronics shop to buy a birthday gift for Carver. We walked up and down the aisles, looking at phones, and headphones, and game players, and cameras.

"What do you think Carver would like?" Dad asked.

"Hmmm . . ." I thought about it. "I'm not sure."

Dad frowned at me. "You should have thought about it, Gabe. It's the last minute. You need to start thinking about things in advance."

"You're definitely right, Dad," I said. "But—"

Dad picked up something from the tabletop display. "Carver is a lot like you, right? Then I know he'll like this a lot."

He held it up to me. A smart watch.

I thought about my watch. I carefully rewrapped it with new paper last night and hid it back in the closet with my other gifts.

A smart watch for Carver?

He'll be careful with it, I told myself.

I was desperate for a gift. The party was only a few hours away.

"Yes. That's a terrific idea, Dad," I said.

That afternoon, Carver met me at the door to his house. He slapped his forehead. "I don't believe it!" he said. "Gabe, you are the first one to arrive!"

"It's the new me," I said. "Always on time."

His eyes went to the gift-wrapped present in my hand. I handed it to him. "Happy birthday," I said.

He studied it. "Hey, thanks. What is it?"

"Go ahead. Open it," I told him.

He ripped away the wrapping. "Oh, wow!" he exclaimed. "Totally awesome! My own smart watch! Awesome!"

He tore it out of the plastic package and started to wrap the band around his wrist. His hand slipped, and he let out a cry. "Oh no! I *dropped* it! Oh, wow. I think it broke."

OUR LITTLE MONSTERS

When my brother, Bill, and I were in middle school, we used to babysit for our little cousins, Eddie and Jon. They were nice boys, but as soon as their parents left the house, they'd climb on Bill and me and wrestle us and pound us and punch and beat us to a pulp.

When their parents returned and asked, "How were the boys?" we always said, "Oh, they were wonderful." Then Bill and I would limp home, beaten and bruised.

I've always thought babysitting was a dangerous job.

I remembered my two little cousins when I thought of this story.

"OW! DON'T BITE!"

I shoved my brother Sean away with both hands. But the little monster dove for me again, snapping his little teeth and giggling.

I grabbed him by the shoulders and held him away. "I'm warning you," I said. "I'll bite back!"

That made him and Chloe howl with laughter. This is what happens whenever Mom and Dad go out and leave me in charge of the twins. They're wild and ferocious and out of control, and they like to gang up on me.

They're four years old and small for their age. And I'm twelve and the tallest girl in my sixth-grade class. But, trust me, when it comes to Sean and Chloe, size doesn't matter.

With a cry of attack, Sean grabbed me around the neck

and pulled my head down to the couch arm. "Hey—don't take my head off!" I cried.

They both thought that was a riot. They have shrill little laughs. It sounds like chipmunks giggling.

I grabbed Sean around the waist and lifted the little guy into the air. He kicked and squirmed. "Put me down! Put me down, Becka!"

Chloe sank her teeth into my leg, and I nearly dropped Sean. They're both terrible biters. When I tell Mom what they do to me, she just says, "Deal with it."

I lowered Sean to the floor and picked up Chloe. "No more biting. I'll have to put you on a leash." I smoothed back her curly brown hair. It looks like poodle fur. The twins aren't identical. Sean has straight black hair and big black eyes.

"Can we stay up late and wrestle some more?" Sean asked.

Before I could answer, my phone rang. Chloe tried to grab it, but I swiped it away from her. It was my friend Izzy. Her real name is Isabella, but even her parents call her Izzy.

"What's up?" Izzy asked.

"I can't talk," I said. "I'm watching the twins."

"You're going to get a medal," she replied. "For bravery."

"They're not that bad," I said.

"Oh, really?" Izzy knows how berserk the twins can be. "I don't know how you babysit them. I think all kids should be locked in a closet until they're at least ten."

"You're sick," I said. "I think—" I didn't finish my sentence. I let out a cry. "Oh NO! Gotta go!" And I clicked off the phone.

I leaped off the couch and went racing to the kitchen. Too late. Sean and Chloe had found the big bowl of chocolate cake batter Mom prepared this morning. And they were already digging their hands into the bowl and heaving big gobs of chocolate at each other.

"Stop! Stop it!" I shouted.

Splaaaat.

A wet gob of cake batter smacked my forehead. The batter oozed down my nose and cheeks.

That caused a burst of chipmunk laughter. And another blob of batter came flying at me. I ducked and it splattered on the carpet.

"Hey—stop! No more!" I begged.

I dove to the kitchen table and reached for the bowl of cake batter. I plunged my hand into the bowl, raised a big handful of chocolate—and smeared it all over Chloe's forehead.

Sean laughed and ducked away. But he wasn't fast enough. I pushed a big hunk of batter onto his nose and wiped it over his cheeks.

All three of us were laughing now and having the best chocolate cake battle ever. *Go with the flow.* That's how I deal with the twins. And we always have the best time together.

By the time Mom and Dad got home, the twins were sound asleep in their beds. I had cleaned up all the globs and chunks of cake batter. Made it all into a cake. And I had the cake baking in the oven.

Dad took a long sip from his water bottle. "How were Sean and Chloe?" he asked.

"They were angels," I said.

Dad spit his water into the air. He and Mom both burst out laughing. They know what the twins are really like.

"If you can handle those two," Mom said, "you could handle anyone. Becka, you're a terrific babysitter."

And that's when I got the idea. I knew how I could earn some spending money and use my talents at the same time. "Mom, what if I got babysitting jobs?" I asked. "I'm old enough, and you just said how good I am at it."

She and Dad exchanged glances. "I guess you could find some jobs here in the neighborhood," Mom said. "But it's hard work, Becka."

"I don't think so," I said. "I think little kids are fun."

I suddenly felt very excited by the idea. What could go wrong?

The next day, I talked about it with Izzy in the lunchroom at school. When I told her my idea, she dropped her peanut butter sandwich on the table. "Don't you have enough of a workout from the twins?" she asked. "Do you seriously like torture?"

"I don't think it's torture," I said. "You just play with the kids. Let them go a little nuts. Wear them out and put them to bed."

Izzy shuddered. "I think little kids should be kept in jars and only taken out at mealtimes."

I laughed. "Why am I starting to get the idea you don't like kids?"

"I like them fried on a bun with special sauce."

Izzy is a real comedian. I mean, she's funny all the time.

"Listen. You could come with me," I said. "We could babysit together and split the money. That would be fun."

She took a big bite of her sandwich. "You're joking, right?"

"Okay, okay. Don't come," I said. "But how do you think I find jobs? Mom and Dad don't want to drive me anywhere. So it has to be in the neighborhood."

"We could print out little posters or signs," Izzy said. "Maybe put them in some of the shops on Main Street. Or maybe on mailboxes or telephone poles."

"That might work," I replied. "What should they say?"

"Insane Person Looking for Torture by Little Monsters," Izzy suggested.

"I like it," I said.

We both laughed.

That night, I wrote a sign and printed it out. I kept it simple. I just wrote: "NEIGHBORHOOD BABYSITTER. Good with all kids. Lots of experience." And I put my phone number at the bottom.

I printed a big stack of them in a bold black font. I thought they looked very professional.

On Saturday, Izzy helped me take them around to some of the little shops on Main Street. And we taped a bunch of them to poles along the sidewalks.

"Lots of kids in this neighborhood," Izzy said. "Your phone will probably start ringing before you even get home."

But she was wrong.

No one called. I kept my phone with me day and night. I kept taking it out and staring at it. I guess I was *willing* it to ring. But it didn't.

A week went by. And then two. And I didn't get a single phone call.

I was about to give up on the whole idea when I stumbled onto my first job.

I was walking home after school with Izzy. It was a gray day with dark storm clouds hanging low overhead. "Is today Friday the thirteenth?" I asked her. "Because I've been unlucky all day."

Izzy frowned at me. "Spilling chocolate milk on your new white sweater wasn't bad luck. It was just klutziness," she said.

"You're always such a good friend," I said. "Where would I be without you there to tell me what a loser I am?"

She stopped and grabbed my arm. "I think your luck is about to change, Becka."

I followed her gaze to the house high on a lawn behind ragged hedges. The Butcher House. Everyone called it that. I don't know why. Maybe someone named Butcher lived there sometime.

It was an empty, abandoned house. No one had lived in it for maybe a hundred years. It was big and dark and stained and crumbling, with broken shingles and missing shutters, and shattered glass in a lot of the windows.

I saw a man and woman on the tilting front stoop. The woman was struggling with a key, trying to open the front door. "Someone is moving into the Butcher House," I said. "How is that going to change my luck?"

Izzy pointed to the side of the stoop. "Check that out."

I saw a small bike and two little silver scooters. "Kids!" I said. "They have kids."

"And they are just moving in," Izzy said. "They're going to need a babysitter." She gave me a push. "Go talk to them. Go tell them you can babysit for them."

I held back. "They're just moving in. They probably don't want to be bothered."

She gave me another push. "This is your big chance, Becka. Be bold."

"Come with me," I said. "We can—"

"No. You have to do this," she replied. "Besides, I'm late for my cello lesson."

Izzy's cello is as big as she is, but she's a talented player.

"Okay, okay," I said, suddenly feeling a fluttering in my chest. "See you tomorrow."

She gave me a wave, shifted the backpack on her back, then hurried away. I took a deep breath and made my way over the weed-choked front lawn to the house.

The woman had just managed to open the front door and was about to go inside when she saw me. They both turned. The man wore a gray hoodie pulled down over black overalls. He was pale and very thin, with gray slits for eyes and a serious expression.

The woman had short, straight black hair and dark eyes. She was also very pale, which made her deep purple lipstick seem to pop off her face. A long, beaded earring dangled from one ear.

"Hi!" I called, a little too loudly. I stopped at the bottom of the stoop. "Are you moving in?" Why did I ask that? Of *course* they were!

"Trying to," the man said without smiling. He had a thin, whispery voice.

"I'm Becka Martin," I said. "I live on the next block. And—"

"We don't know the neighborhood at all," the woman said. "We're new in town."

"It looks nice here," the man said. "Very quiet."

"It's pretty quiet," I said. "It's like . . . a normal neighborhood." *Awkward.* I pointed to the bike and the scooters. "You have kids?"

They glanced at each other, as if trying to decide how to answer. The woman tugged at her dangling earring. "Two kids. Four and five."

"Well . . ." I took another deep breath. "If you ever need a babysitter . . ."

They both blinked. The man squinted hard at me, as if studying me.

The woman smiled for the first time. "Would you really like to come and babysit our little monsters?"

I laughed. "My little brother and sister are monsters, too," I said. "So I have experience. And I really like little kids."

"Let me get them," the woman said. She pushed open the heavy front door and disappeared inside.

The man scratched the side of his face with one hand and continued to stare at me. He started to say something, but then stopped. I decided he must be shy.

The woman appeared a few seconds later, pushing two kids in front of her. She kept a hand on their shoulders as if holding them in place. They were both as pale as the parents.

The girl wore a dark blue jumper over black tights. Her straight black hair fell loosely down her back. The boy had on a floppy black T-shirt and black shorts. I guessed that the girl was the older one. But they were both small for their age.

"This is Gorm," the woman said, tapping the girl's shoulder. "And this is Garg." She patted the boy.

"Strange names," I blurted out.

"They're old family names," the woman said.

"What's *your* name?" the little girl demanded.

"Becka," I answered.

"Strange name," she said. Her brother laughed.

"Would you like Becka to come stay with you some night?" the mother asked.

"No!" both kids declared at once.

"Of course you do," the father spoke up in his whispery voice. He turned to me. "They're both very shy around strangers."

"No we're not," Gorm said.

I laughed. "Gorm, I think we're going to be good friends," I said, flashing her a warm smile.

I'm not sure exactly what happened next.

I'm pretty sure I imagined it. I saw a black spot move on the floor of the stoop. A big spider. And I'm not sure, but I think I saw Garg reach down and pick the spider up between his fingers—and pop it into his mouth.

I blinked a few times. It was shadowy on the porch because of the storm clouds up above. But I did see the little boy chewing something, chewing pretty hard, and I'm pretty sure it was the spider.

These kids might be trouble, I thought.

But I reminded myself how desperate I was to have a job.

"Becka, can you come babysit them tomorrow night?" the woman asked.

"Yes," I replied. "No problem."

"I'm warning you, don't smear that peanut butter on me!"

The next afternoon, Izzy and I were watching the twins

until my parents returned home from grocery shopping. As always, their idea of fun was making a mess.

Sean giggled like a mad fiend and raised the glob of peanut butter in front of my face. "Dare me?"

"No. I don't dare you!" I cried. "I'm warning you—"

Smussh. He slapped the peanut butter onto my forehead. I let out an angry cry. Sean and Chloe tossed back their heads and laughed as if it was the funniest thing they'd ever seen.

I grabbed the sticky blob off my forehead and tossed it at Sean. He dodged to the side, and it flew onto the carpet. Now it was Chloe's turn to come at me with a handful of peanut butter.

I tried to grab her, but she was too fast for me. "Not my hair! Not my hair!" I screamed.

She shot her hand forward and rubbed it down the side of my hair. I screamed again, jumped to my feet, and shoved her away.

Izzy sat across the room with her phone in her hands. "Becka, how can you even *think* of babysitting?" she demanded. "These twins should be arrested and kept in prison for life."

I ran to the kitchen to get a wet paper towel to try to wipe the peanut butter from my hair. "I don't think the other kids will be this much trouble," I said. "They seem very shy and quiet."

Izzy tsk-tsked. "You're in major trouble. You should bring a dog crate with you to use as a cage. Just in case."

I rolled my eyes. "Very funny. Know what? I'm glad you're not coming along."

I screamed as Sean sank his teeth into my wrist. "No biting! No biting!" I cried. "Remember—I can bite back!"

The evening sun was sinking behind the trees when I showed up at the Butcher House for my job. I was surprised to see the house completely dark, no lights on anywhere.

The floorboards on the front stoop creaked as I walked up to the front door. It swung open before I could knock. The woman smiled at me. Her pale face was gray in the dim light. She wore a loose black sweater over a long black skirt.

She held the door open, and I slipped past her into the front room. "Right on time," she said. "Thank you for coming."

It took a while for my eyes to adjust to the dim light. I saw a few large cartons piled in the center of the room. Otherwise, the room was completely bare.

"Our furniture hasn't arrived," she said, reading my thoughts. "We are trying to track it down. It might be lost."

"Whoa. That's too bad," I murmured.

I heard footsteps on the bare floorboards. The man appeared from a back room. He was also dressed in black. He had a black baseball cap pulled low on his forehead.

"Hello, Becka," he said. "The kids are waiting for you in the playroom." He pointed to a door near the back hall.

"Awesome," I said. "I think we're going to have fun."

They didn't reply to that.

"When is their bedtime?" I asked.

They both shrugged. "Whenever," the man said.

"You'll know when it's time to put them down," the woman added.

I nodded. "Well . . . okay. No worries. Have a nice evening."

"You too." They started to the front door.

"Do you want to leave me a phone number so I could reach you if I have to?" I asked.

"We don't have our phones yet," the woman said.

"No problem. When will you be back?" I asked.

They exchanged glances. "It's a full moon tonight," the man answered. "So we'll be out till after midnight."

Huh? What does that mean?

The door closed behind them before I could ask.

I found the two kids down on the floor in the middle of the next room. It was as bare as the front room. No furniture at all. A floor lamp against one wall gave off pale yellow light.

Garg and Gorm were dressed alike in gray T-shirts and shorts. They were on their knees, each holding a blue helium balloon on a string.

"Hey, guys," I called as I walked over to them. "What's up?"

They stared back at me and didn't reply.

"Remember me? I'm Becka," I said.

Garg lowered his eyes to the floor. Gorm continued to stare at me. "We know," she said softly.

It's going to be hard to get a conversation going with these two, I thought.

"Tell me, guys," I said, "have you had dinner?"

"Not yet," Gorm replied.

"Not yet?" I repeated. "Well, what are you going to have for dinner?"

"You," Garg said. They both laughed, chirpy little laughs.

"No. Really," I said.

"Really," Garg replied, and they both laughed again.

Better change the subject, Becka, I told myself. I pointed to their balloons. "Are you playing a game with those?"

Gorm swept back her straight black hair. "No. We're not playing a game."

"We're just hitting each other with them," Garg said. He swung the string and bounced his balloon off Gorm's head. She swung back and bumped her balloon over Garg's face.

"That isn't much fun," I said. "Do you know how to play volleyball with a balloon? We could bat it back and forth—"

"We don't want to," Garg said. He swung the string again and bounced the balloon off his sister's head.

"Oh!" they both cried out as the string slipped from Garg's hand. The balloon floated up. He grabbed for the string and missed. The three of us watched his balloon hit the ceiling high above us.

Garg made a pouty face and beat his fists against the floor.

"Oh, wow. Too bad," I said. I gazed up at the balloon bouncing lightly against the ceiling. "Do you have a ladder? Maybe I could climb up and get it."

"We don't need a ladder," Garg said. He jumped to his feet and walked to the wall. Then he did a backflip until his shoes were flat against the wall.

And he walked up the side of the wall!

I let out a startled cry. "How did you *do* that? Come down! Come down, Garg! You'll fall on your head!"

Gorm laughed. She flipped herself sideways and walked up the wall. She joined her brother on the ceiling. He grabbed his balloon. Then they both lowered themselves—and hung by their legs, upside down from the high rafter.

"Come down!" I shrieked. "Come down—*now!*"

"Come up here and *make* us!" Gorm shouted.

"I can't!" I told her. "I can't climb walls. How did you do that?"

They both laughed in reply. "Come down," I repeated. "Let's play another game. Let's play something more fun."

They whispered to each other. Then they both swung off the rafter and walked down the wall.

"Whew." I breathed a sigh of relief. What if one of them had fallen?

They joined me in the middle of the floor. "We know a good game," Garg said.

Gorm nodded. "It's called Bite-Bite."

"Never heard of it," I said. "How do you play it?"

"I told you, we didn't have dinner," Garg said, bumping up close to me.

"So Bite-Bite is a good game to play," his sister added.

"Huh?" I squinted at them.

"It's easy to play," Garg said. "We just bite you."

"You're joking, right?" I said. I pushed him away. "You kids are weird."

"Yes, we're weird," Gorm agreed.

Then I uttered a cry as the two of them started to change. Their eyes turned red and bulged until they poked out like Ping-Pong balls. Their noses stretched into long snouts. Thick brown fur sprouted over their faces. And curled, yellow fangs dropped from their open mouths.

Their chests heaved in and out, and they started to make animal grunts. Drool oozed down their yellow fangs.

"No!" I screamed. "No! No! Noooo! Your parents didn't lie. You really ARE little monsters!"

They both snapped their teeth at me. I tried to back away, but I was trapped. Uttering low growls, they snapped again.

"Stop!" I cried. "Stop! When your parents get home, I'm going to tell them you didn't behave."

Both little monsters tossed back their fur-covered heads and laughed.

"Wh-what's so funny?" I stammered.

"They're not coming home," Garg grunted. "They're never coming back."

"Huh? No—" I started.

"They're not our parents," Gorm said. "They couldn't wait to escape. They brought you here so they could get away."

"No! No way—!" I gasped.

"They told you we were little monsters, but you didn't listen," Gorm growled.

"Now we're *very* hungry," Garg said. "Sorry, but we have to play serious Bite-Bite!"

Grunting and snapping their teeth, they moved in on me. I had my back pressed against the wall. Nowhere to move. I jerked my arm away just as Garg leaped up to bite me.

"I—I'm warning you—" I cried. "I bite back!"

They both laughed ugly, deep laughs. Garg jumped again and nipped my elbow.

"Ouch! Okay—that's it for you two!" I shouted.

I let out a roar and swept a hand back over my head. I felt my jaws begin to slide forward. It took only a second for my alligator-long snout to stretch. I tested my four rows of jagged teeth.

I roared again as curled claws poked from my growing hands, and the fur sprouted over my face, my arms, my legs.

Garg and Gorm uttered startled cries. They tried to back away, but I was too fast for them. With an animal bleat of triumph, I clamped my alligator jaws over both of them—caught them both at once—and bit down hard.

At home, I introduced Gorm and Garg to *our* little monsters, Chloe and Sean. The four of them leaped on one another, growling and nipping, rolling around and wrestling like little monsters love to do.

Mom picked up the new arrivals in her giant paws and petted them tenderly. She rolled her three eyes. "Two more mouths to feed tonight," she murmured. "That's a lot of raw meat."

Then Mom turned to me. "Becka, do me a favor," she said. "Don't take any more babysitting jobs."

SKIN

Once, at an animal preserve in Tucson, I watched a snake shed its skin. The snake slithered right out as if it was taking off a winter coat. The skin had been a part of the creature, and now it was just a long, paper-thin crusty thing I could see through.

That image stayed with me a long time.

Lots of scary stories have been written about snakes. But I've never read a story about their skin. And then I suddenly had this story idea about a boy and his skin.

MY DAD ALWAYS SAYS, "YOU CAN BE WHOEVER YOU WANT TO BE."
I'm Freddy Baker, and right now, I want to be the best
thirteen-year-old basketball player in history.

I know. That's never going to happen. But it's good to
have big goals, don't you think? Right now, right at this
moment, I'm dribbling down the gym floor, feeling confi-
dent, feeling like I have it all.

My middle school team, the Rattlers, is down by
only one point, and there's twenty seconds left in the
game. Everyone on the bleachers is screaming, on their
feet, jumping up and down. The bleachers are actually
bouncing, and the sound of the screams and cheers rings
off the high gym ceiling.

Everyone knows I'm going to drive into the paint and
end the game with an easy layup, and the Red Hawks will
lose with no time left. Baker the Playmaker wins another

game for the Rattlers, and it's on to the state champion-ship game in Grover City.

Here I go, dodging the red uniforms, sliding away from two slapping hands, thundering toward the basket. Here's my winning shot. I can hear the screams and cries grow louder.

Oh, wow. No. Oh no.

My hand—it slipped. The ball sailed off. It hit the bottom of the backboard and bounced out of bounds.

The screams stopped as if someone had clicked off the volume. Groans and moans drowned out the final buzzer.

I missed. We lost. We lost the game to the Red Hawks because my hand slipped. Baker the Playmaker is a loser today.

The Red Hawk guys are celebrating, bumping high-fives and jumping up and down, chest bumps and a lot of roaring. I follow my guys off the floor. The sweat feels cold on my face. I keep my head down. I don't want to see my teammates. I let them down.

My friend Jackson jumps up from the bottom row of the bleachers. He walks over and puts a hand on my shoulder. "Hey, there's one more game next week," he says. "Not your fault, Freddy."

Of *course* it's my fault. I blew the easy shot. I brush Jackson's hand off my shoulder and slump into the locker room.

Almost silent in here. I hear the slam of lockers and water dribbling in the shower room. I slump onto a bench and wait for my breathing to slow to normal. I'm drenched in cold sweat, but I don't feel like taking a shower. A few guys nod at me, but the others are definitely avoiding me.

How did the ball slip like that? I raise my shooting hand and examine it.

Whoa. Weird. The skin feels loose.

I move it around with my other hand. The skin on my fingers definitely feels loose, as if it doesn't fit my hand anymore. *Maybe I'm dehydrated*, I tell myself. *I have to drink more water.*

I found Jackson waiting for me in front of the playground. He saw the upset look on my face. "Don't get down, Freddy," he said. "You scored twenty-two points, more than anyone else in the game."

"I don't want to talk about it," I said. I'm not a crier. I never cry. So why was my voice breaking up?

Jackson gave me a shove toward the street. "Let's go. Grow up," he said.

I pushed back. "Do you know how helpful you're being? Not helpful."

He tossed his hands up. "Okay, okay. So you weren't Baker the Playmaker today. So—"

"I was Baker the Game Loser," I groaned. "It doesn't even rhyme."

That made him laugh. "Well . . . nothing rhymes with Jackson," he said. "That's why I don't play basketball."

"You don't play basketball because you're a total klutz," I said.

"That too," he said. "I told Melody we'd meet her at your parents' place."

My parents own a little lunch diner two blocks from the school where a lot of kids hang out. It's tiny. It has a long counter with stools and four booths against the wall.

There's an ancient *Pac-Man* arcade game at the back that belonged to my grandfather. It sends a constant *ping ping ping* sound over the tiny place.

Melody was waiting for us at the counter with a pink smoothie in a tall glass in front of her. She was wearing a red-and-yellow Rattlers jersey and a short gray skirt over black leggings.

She turned when Jackson and I walked in. Her dark hair was tied behind her in a red scrunchie. Melody has narrow dark eyes that always seem to be studying you.

Jackson and I dropped down on stools on either side of her. The booths were filled with kids, and a group of teenagers huddled around the *Pac-Man* machine in back.

"Why weren't you at the game?" I asked.

"I didn't want to watch you lose," she replied.

"Ooh, that's cold!" Jackson cried. "That's seriously *cold*."

"How'd you know we lost?" I demanded.

"Actually, I was there," Melody said. She took a long sip on the straw. "I didn't think you'd want to talk about it."

"You got that right," I said.

Norman Washburn appeared behind the counter with a tray of glasses in his hands. My parents stay home on weekends and leave the lunch counter to Norman. He's pretty old, with wavy white hair that he never brushes and cheeks that are always red.

"Hey, dudes, what'll you have?" Norman always tries to talk like he's a young person. "Cherry colas?"

He knows that's what Jackson and I always get. He set the tray of glasses down, leaned close, and squinted at me. "Hey, Freddy, better show me your money first."

It's the same joke every time. He knows I don't have to pay. "Charge it," I said. It wasn't that funny, but he laughed.

I turned back to my friends. In a flash, I saw my missed layup again and heard the disappointed groans of the people in the bleachers. *Am I going to see that missed shot forever?*

Jackson knew what I was thinking. "We still have the game with the Hornets next week," he said.

Melody sipped her drink. "Let's not talk about it. Let's talk about our overnight in Jefferson Woods. That was so nice of your parents to invite Jackson and me."

I shook my head. "I didn't want to go. I think the woods

are boring, and I don't like sleeping outside at night." I shuddered. "Too many bugs."

"It'll be an adventure," Jackson said.

"Take your mind off what a loser you are," Melody said.

She and Jackson laughed. He likes her cruel sense of humor.

"They're doing it for Willy," I said. Willy is my little brother. "He's seriously weird," I said. "When it's warm, he sleeps in the backyard in a tent."

"Your brother is cool," Melody said. "I think—"

She didn't finish because Norman appeared with our cherry colas in tall glasses. "Watch out for the bubbles," he said. He always says that. He set the two glasses in front of me and hurried to a man waving at him at the other end of the counter.

"Here you go." I picked up Jackson's drink and reached past Melody to hand it to him. But—whoa! Oh no! The glass slipped from my hand—and fell into Melody's lap.

She screamed. We both made grabs for it. But the dark cola splashed all over her skirt and Rattlers jersey, and the glass hit the floor and shattered into pieces.

Melody grabbed a paper napkin and swiped frantically at her skirt as the cola soaked over the front. "I don't *believe* you!" she screamed at me. "Did you do that on purpose? Because I made fun of you?"

"No! No way!" I cried. I saw Norman bringing a towel to help mop up the spill. "My hand slipped. I—"

I gazed at my hand. Oh, wow. The skin on my fingers was loose. The skin dangled like a glove falling off.

With a gasp, I frantically pulled the skin back onto my fingers. Did Melody and Jackson see it? No. She was on her feet now, her shoes crinkling over the broken glass, swiping the towel at the front of her skirt.

Jackson had jumped to his feet, too. He stared at me as if he was trying to figure out what was going on with me.

I shrugged. "Guess I'm just a total klutz today," I said. I was trying to keep it light, but my skin had me really worried.

At dinner, my family talked about our overnight. Willy kept asking if he could have his own tent. Dad laughed. "Why don't you want to sleep with Freddy?"

"I just want my own tent," the little guy answered.

"Then I'll have to sleep out in the open," I said, "and maybe a bear will come and eat me."

"That's why I want to be in a tent!" Willy said.

Mom and Dad laughed. They think Willy is a riot, and I guess he is.

I wasn't in a laughing mood. I was still thinking about the basketball game I lost for my team. "If only my hand hadn't slipped," I told my parents. "We would have won."

"Listen to me, Freddy," Dad said. He has a big, booming voice, and you have to listen to him when he speaks. "It takes five players to lose a game, not just one."

I guess he was saying I shouldn't blame myself. But, of course, I did.

"Can we go tubing on the Jefferson River?" Willy asked.

"It's too cold," Mom said.

"Not for *me*!" Willy exclaimed.

Dad put a hand over Willy's mouth. "I'm talking to Freddy," he said. He turned back to me. "Forget about the game today. You have to keep plugging, and don't look back."

"I know," I said. "But—"

"You can do it, Freddy," Dad boomed. "Remember what I always say—you can be whoever you want to be."

"Why does Freddy get to bring his friends?" Willy said. "Why can't I?"

"You don't have any friends," I said.

Mom scowled at me. "Don't pick on your brother, Freddy."

She always takes his side.

Later, I decided to take a hot shower before bed. As

I walked to the bathroom, I stopped in front of the one weird thing in my house. Believe me, my parents are totally normal people. They are hardworking and serious, and they are really good parents.

But there's one thing in our house that anyone would think is seriously strange. We call it the Forbidden Closet. It's the closet next to the upstairs bathroom. The door is locked with a padlock, and no one is allowed to open it.

No matter how many times I've asked about it, I can't get an answer from either Mom or Dad about why it's forbidden and what is inside it. They always make a zipping motion in front of their mouths and say, "My lips are sealed."

So, it's just a part of our house, a forbidden closet. Willy and I pass it several times a day, and we don't even think about it anymore.

I took a long, hot shower. I thought it might help me calm down. Afterward, I grabbed a bath towel from the racks on the wall and started to dry myself.

"Whoa!" I uttered a cry as the towel slipped from my hands.

I made a grab for the towel, but I saw something was wrong. The skin on both hands was loose, dangling off my fingers. It was as if my skin didn't fit me anymore.

I don't know how long I just stood there, dripping wet, my hands raised in front of me, staring at the flopping, loose skin.

"This is *sick*!" I cried out loud.

I worked frantically to pull the skin back onto my fingers. It wasn't easy since both hands were messed up. Then I dried myself quickly, tugged on my pajamas, and hurried downstairs.

After dinner, Mom had gone to her sister's house. But Dad was in the den, reading a magazine called *Restaurant Life*. I burst up in front of him and lowered the magazine to his lap.

"Dad, there's something wrong with me!" I cried. "My—my skin is coming loose! My hands—the skin is sliding off my hands. Something is terribly wrong!"

To my surprise, he didn't react at all. He leaned forward in his armchair, reached up to his ears, and pulled out the wireless earbuds. He squinted at me. "Sorry, Freddy. Did you say something? I had Led Zeppelin in my ears. That old stuff helps clear my head."

"I, uh . . ." I tugged at my fingers to show him the problem. But the skin stayed in place. I tugged hard, but the skin didn't come loose.

"Something wrong with your hand?" Dad said. "You have another hangnail?"

"N-no," I stammered. "I guess I'm okay. I just came down to say good night."

Saturday morning before the basketball game, I was down on the living room floor, playing a game with Willy. Playing games with Willy isn't exactly fun because he cheats. And if he loses, he goes berserk and messes up the board and starts heaving game pieces all over the room.

We were playing Connect Four. He had three of his red checkers in a row and jumped up and down, saying he had won.

I pulled him back down. "You need *four* in a row," I said. "The game is called Connect Four."

"No, it isn't," Willy insisted. He gave me a hard shove. "It's called Connect THREE."

I stabbed my finger against the front of the game box. "See this number? It's a four. You need four in a row, not three. Don't be a cheater."

"*You're* the cheater!" he cried. He shoved the game onto its side and tossed some checkers against the wall.

I stood the game back up. "Let's start again," I said quietly. "Do you want to play Connect Three? Okay. We can play Connect Three."

Willy squinted at me for a long moment. Then he burst out laughing.

"What's so funny?" I said.

"Your face," he answered.

I let out an exasperated breath. "Are we going to play or not?"

He pointed. "How do you do that, Freddy?"

"Do what?"

"How do you do that with your face? It's totally weird!"

"Huh?" I jumped up and went running to the bathroom. I stepped up to the sink and leaned close to the mirror. *What is Willy laughing about?*

I gasped when I saw the reflection of my ears. The skin on both my ears dangled down the sides of my face. It looked like my ears were hanging down to my shoulders!

"How do you do that?" I heard Willy coming down the hall.

I wrapped my fingers around my ear skin and pushed it back into place. Then I spun around as Willy burst into the bathroom. "Do *what*?" I said.

The basketball game was a disaster.

I kept slipping as I ran down the floor. I had to stop and see if my sneakers had come unlaced. My legs felt wobbly, as if my bones had turned soft or something. I went up for a long three-pointer and fell flat on my face. I landed hard on my elbows, and pain shot up and down my whole body.

Whistles blew. Coach Franklin shouted for a time-out and waved me over. He frowned at me as I stumbled over to him. "What's up, Freddy?"

"I—I'm okay," I stammered. "I—I think it's my shoes."

He put a hand on my shoulder and gave me a gentle push toward the sideline. "Take some bench time and check it out."

My heart started to pound as I dropped onto the bench. I had a bad feeling the problem wasn't my sneakers. I held my breath and hoped I was wrong.

Both sneakers were tightly laced. My hands trembled as I pulled off the left sneaker. "Oh, wow," I murmured to myself. I slid off the other sneaker and gazed in horror at my feet.

I heard the crowd cheering and shouting, but their voices seemed miles away.

The skin had drooped off both my feet. The toes dangled limply. The skin was at least two inches off the bone.

I forced myself to breathe. My eyes blurred as I stared at the loose skin.

What is happening?

I saw Coach Franklin approaching. No time to tug the skin back into place. Frantically, I tried to stuff my feet back into the sneakers. I jammed them in and struggled to lace them back up with my shaking hands.

"Everything check out?" Coach Franklin asked.

I nodded. "I guess."

He blew his whistle. "Get back in, Freddy. Let's beat these guys."

I jumped up, started to run onto the floor—and fell again. My feet just didn't fit in the shoes. Whistles blew again. The crowd grew silent. Coach Franklin squatted down beside me. "Do you need help?"

"N-no," I stammered. I pulled myself to a sitting position. "Just not feeling well. Sorry, Coach. I'd better not play today."

Stumbling and staggering, I made my way home, eager to tell my parents about my loose skin. I found them in the driveway, packing the van for the overnight.

Dad shoved a tent into the back and turned to me, a look of surprise on his face. "Freddy? You're home early?"

"I need to talk—" I started.

But then Melody and Jackson stepped out from behind

the van. I stopped midsentence. I didn't want them to know what was happening to me.

"Who won the game?" Jackson asked.

"Later," I said. "I . . . uh . . . I have to pack some things." I hurried into the house. I needed to talk to Mom and Dad, but not in front of my friends.

My shoes wobbled on my feet as I started up the stairs to my room. I spun around when I heard footsteps behind me and saw Jackson following. "Freddy, what's up with you?" he demanded. "Is something wrong?"

"I . . . don't want to talk about it," I said. I hurried the rest of the way up. "I just want to get my backpack and—"

"Hey, what's this?" he asked. "Why is there a padlock on this door?"

I groaned. "Don't worry about it," I said.

"No. Seriously," Jackson said. He tugged at the padlock. "What's in here?"

"Didn't I ever tell you about it?" I said. "It's the Forbidden Closet."

He squinted at me. "You're joking."

I shook my head. "No one is allowed to open it," I told him. "It's forbidden."

Jackson laughed. "This is definitely weird. Aren't you curious about it? Have you ever tried to look inside?"

"No. Come on, Jackson. We're in a hurry."

He pulled something from his jeans pocket. I think

it was a nail clipper. "I learned how to pick locks from a YouTube video," he said. "Let's take a look here." He went to work on the lock.

I grabbed his arm. But he pulled it free and kept picking at the padlock. "We've got to find out what is so forbidden," he said. "Hey—I think I've got it!"

"What are you guys doing?" a voice called. Dad appeared at the top of the stairs. "Get a move on, Freddy. Get your stuff. I don't want to drive after dark."

We arrived at Jefferson Woods at twilight. It was a cool night. The air smelled fresh and piney. A pale half-moon was hanging just over the trees. A steady breeze made the leaves whisper above our heads.

Dad and Jackson started to set up the tents. "Do mine first!" Willy cried. "Me first!" He pointed to a row of low shrubs. "Over there. I want it over there."

"At least you're not bossy," I said.

"Don't pick on Willy," Mom said. "Let's have a fun night, Freddy."

"You and Melody go gather firewood before it gets totally dark," Dad said. "We need to build a big fire."

Melody turned and began walking into the trees beyond

the clearing. I started after her, but I stumbled over a fallen tree limb and fell to the ground.

I heard Willy laughing behind me. I didn't think it was funny. My feet still didn't feel right in my shoes.

Melody helped me up. "Let's collect kindling first," she said. "There are sticks all over the ground. Then we can come back for bigger pieces of wood."

"Sounds like a plan," I said. We wandered off in different directions. I nearly walked into a hedge of thick nettles. Catching my balance just in time, I leaned against a fat tree trunk.

The bark felt rough against my back. I saw a bunch of thin twigs at my feet. I bent and tried to gather them up. "Whoa!" The twigs slipped right through my fingers.

I swiped at them again. Missed. A wave of dizziness made me lean back against the tree. The woods seemed to grow silent. I blinked as the gray evening light faded in front of me.

"Ow." I swiped at a mosquito on my neck. And felt the loose skin under my chin. "Oh no." A frightened moan escaped my throat.

I grabbed the sides of my face. The skin on my cheeks was flapping loose.

This can't be happening.
This is impossible!

My fingers dangled off my hands. I tried to press them against the front of my sweatshirt. But my whole chest was moving!

I raised my hands to my head and pulled. My skin slid up over my face. My skin . . . my skin . . . my skin . . . it was sliding off!

All of it. All of my skin. It came off in one long piece. Like a Halloween costume. Came off in my hands.

Gasping for breath, my chest heaving up and down, horrified groans escaped my throat. Animal grunts. And there I was, leaning against the rough tree bark, my skin draped over my arm like a long towel.

I reached up with my free hand. Reached up to my face.

Do I have a face?

Yes. I felt my cheeks, my forehead. I had a face under my old face!

"No . . . no . . . no . . ." Was that *me* groaning and repeating that word?

I gripped my skin tightly against me. A shrill scream of horror made me almost drop it.

Melody stood open-mouthed, gaping at me. She screamed again and took a step back, her eyes wide with fright.

"Who *are* you?" she cried. "What are you doing here in the woods?"

"It's . . . me . . ." I tried to answer. But the words came out in a choked whisper.

"What have you done to Freddy?" Melody cried, hands pressed to her cheeks. "Why are you wearing Freddy's clothes? Where is he? Who *are* you?"

"It's me . . ." I croaked.

"No! Where is Freddy?" Melody cried. "Where is he?" And then she opened her mouth in another horrified scream, so loud it made the trees shake.

I shut my eyes and covered my ears against her screams. *Who am I now?* I wondered. *If I'm not Freddy, who am I now?*

"I thought this might happen," Dad said. He took my skin, rolled it up, and shoved it into the back of the van. "Get in, everyone. We have to go home."

We drove home in silence. I sat up front with Dad and stared out into the darkness. Melody and Jackson sat with Mom. I could feel them staring at me—the stranger in the car!

Willy started to whine about how he didn't want to leave the woods. Dad hushed him up instantly.

At home, Dad unpacked my skin and carried it upstairs.

I followed him, my heart pounding, my brain whirring in confusion. He stopped outside the Forbidden Closet.

"You're thirteen, Freddy," Dad said. "I figured it was time." He spun the wheel on the padlock and tugged it open.

Then he motioned for me to stand back as he swung open the closet door. He clicked on a ceiling light, and I peered inside. And stared at the rows of objects draped over hangers.

"Oh, wow," I gasped. "Are those all human skins?"

Dad nodded. "Pick one, Freddy. Who do you want to be next?"

He reached in and lifted out a hanger. I stared at the skin draped over it. "I used to wear this one," Dad said. "But I shed it before you were born."

"Huh?" I blinked a few times, trying to understand.

"So then I picked the skin I'm wearing now," Dad said, pinching his own cheek.

"But—but—" I sputtered.

Dad smiled and placed a hand on my shoulder. "Freddy, what have I always told you? You can be whoever you want to be!"

THE GHOST
IN THE CAR

This is one of those stories where I didn't have an idea, but I had the title. It happens to me lots of times. A good title for a scary story pops into my head. And the title makes me think about what the story should be about.

And so I began to think about a car with a ghost in it . . .

How would a ghost get into a car?

Why would the ghost stay in the car?

How would the ghost scare the riders in the car?

What does the ghost want?

Then, for some reason, I found myself thinking about my cousin when I was a kid back in Ohio. He had a beat-up car of his own, and he drove me to school and back every day.

I don't know why I started thinking about my cousin. But I put him together with a haunted car—and suddenly I had the plot for this story.

MILLER STEPPED INTO THE HOUSE, AND AVA AND I BOTH GROANED.
I don't know if Miller heard us or not. Ava and I were
never happy to see my cousin. But he's so stuck on himself,
he never guessed that we didn't like him.

Miller thinks everyone is wild about him. But no one is
more wild about Miller than Miller.

He had a wide grin on his face, but it wasn't the kind of
grin that made you happy. It was a grin that said *I'm bad
and I have bad ideas in my head.*

It was a seriously disturbing grin, and Miller grinned a
lot because he was a disturbing kind of guy.

My friend Ava Decker and I had been playing *Minecraft*
on my mom's laptop. But I knew we'd have to stop now
that Miller had arrived.

He stomped up behind me and gave me a hard punch
on the shoulder for no reason. I tried not to cry out, but I

couldn't help it. It hurt. After all, Miller is seventeen, five years older than me, and at least a ton heavier than me. He works out at his dad's gym and considers himself a sports star.

I rubbed my shoulder. "What are you doing here?" I asked him. Okay. That wasn't the friendliest thing to say. But Miller would never notice.

"Staring at your ugly face, Goo-Goo," he replied, the grin even wider.

My name is Paul Goolsby, and he insists on calling me Goo-Goo because he knows I hate it. Who wouldn't hate it?

"Don't call him Goo-Goo," Ava told Miller. She knows it's a waste of time. But she always sticks up for me anyway.

Miller tickled her under the chin. "You're a goo-goo, too."

She jerked her head away from him. "Give us a break, Miller."

He laughed. He has a sick laugh. It sounds like he's choking. "Ava, what do you brush your hair with—a salad fork?" He laughed at his own bad joke.

"At least I have hair," she murmured. Miller's blond hair is shaved so short, it looks like fuzz on a tennis ball.

"I keep my hair short for swim meets," he said, patting his head. "You have to keep it sleek to win competitions."

"You learned how to swim?" I said.

He ignored my joke. He grabbed the laptop screen and swung it toward him. "What game are you two playing?" he demanded. *"Baby's First Loose Tooth?* I hear that's an awesome game."

He grinned at me. "Too hard for you, Goo-Goo?"

I wanted to punch him, but that would be a big mistake. Miller likes to punch back, and his fists are as big as my head. The sad fact is, I'm stuck with him.

He and my aunt and uncle live on the next block, and we see them all the time. Ever since my parents split up, Mom has worked as a substitute teacher. Which means we don't have much money. Miller's dad, my uncle Ralph, owns three gyms in town. He helps Mom and me out a lot.

I even wear Miller's old clothes to school. Some things are too big for me. The jeans are real baggy, and I have to wear a tight belt to keep them up. But what choice do I have?

Ava and I see Miller almost every day. He takes his mom's car, and he drives us to school in the morning and drives us home in the afternoon.

"We're playing *Minecraft*," Ava said.

Miller squinted at the screen. "I could give you some pointers. I won a state championship in *Minecraft*," he bragged.

I could tell he was lying. These little pink circles break

out on his cheeks whenever he tells a lie. Which means he almost always has pink circles on his cheeks.

Besides, who ever heard of a state championship for *Minecraft*?

I turned away from the laptop. "Miller, did you bring back my tablet?" I asked.

"Oops. Forgot," he said.

"You promised you'd return it last week," I told him.

"Forgot," he repeated. "I haven't seen it for a while. Are you sure I didn't already bring it back to you?"

I balled my hands into fists and let out a low growl. "I'm sure," I muttered.

Mom entered the room, carrying a tall stack of old magazines in front of her. "Cleaning out the den," she said. "Why do we keep these old magazines?" Then she saw Miller. "Oh. Hi. I didn't know you were here." She shifted the magazines in her hands. "What's up?"

"Just helping them out with some tips about *Minecraft*," Miller replied. "The game is a lot more fun if you know what you're doing."

"That's nice of you," Mom said. She has *no idea* what Miller is really like. Because he's always sweet and polite whenever he sees her. Mom is really smart. I mean, she's been a teacher her whole career. But she sure is fooled by Miller.

Mom set the magazines down on the coffee table.

"Maybe I should go through them before I toss them out." Then she squinted at Miller. "Hey, wait. Your mom told me you had a big basketball game today. What are you doing here?"

Miller shrugged. "I had to quit the team," he told her. "Actually, they asked me to leave."

Mom's mouth dropped open. "Asked you to leave? Why?"

"Because I'm too good," Miller said. "The other guys on my team couldn't keep up with me. They're just not on the same level as I am."

"That's a shame," Mom said.

I saw the pink circles on Miller's cheeks, and I knew he was lying. But Mom didn't notice them.

"It's no biggie," Miller told her. "Actually, I got tired of having to do all the scoring. I figured the other guys would have more fun if they could play on their own level without me making them look bad all the time."

Miller's cheeks went from pink to red. Was Mom really buying that total load of bull from him?

"You're a good guy," she told him. "Very generous. I hope you can find a better team that will challenge you."

Oh, wow. Ava and I stared at each other. We both knew that Miller had probably been kicked off the team because he was terrible or because he bullied the other players.

Miller invited himself to lunch. Saturday was

homemade pizza day, and Ava and I weren't happy we'd have to share. We sat down around the kitchen table. Miller sat beside me and kept elbowing me in the ribs just for fun. He stopped whenever Mom turned toward us.

"Have you decided anything about college?" Mom asked him, sliding the pizza from the oven. Miller graduated from Crocker High School last spring. He has been taking a year off to "find himself."

"I'm looking at some of the Ivy League colleges in the east," he told her. "A few of them are interested in me."

I watched the pink circles pop up on his cheeks.

"I'm hoping to get a golf scholarship," Miller said.

"I didn't know you play golf," Ava said.

"I'm taking it up this summer," he replied. "After a few weeks, I'm sure I'll be good enough for a scholarship."

Mom dished out two slices of pizza on each plate. It smelled terrific. Mom uses two kinds of cheese and a spicy tomato sauce and little bacon bits. I took a few bites. The pizza was awesome.

"Oh, wait," I said, standing up. "I hear my phone ringing in the other room."

I was gone from the kitchen for only a minute or two. But when I sat back down at the table, there was only one slice on my plate, the slice I'd taken two bites from.

"Hey—where's my other slice?" I cried, turning to Miller beside me.

He grinned while he was chewing. "Huh? What's your problem?"

"Did you eat my other slice?" I demanded.

He swallowed a big mouthful. "No way. Why would I eat your slice?"

I turned to Ava across the table. "Did you see?"

She shook her head. "No. I was looking at my own plate."

"Mom—" I started. But what was the point? She'd never believe that my angel cousin would steal the food off my plate.

Miller laughed and shoved more pizza into his mouth.

After lunch when he was finally leaving, he grabbed my arm really hard and pulled me to the stairs. "Saturday is your allowance day, right?"

I had a bad feeling about that question. "Uh . . . yeah."

"Lend me ten dollars," he whispered, looking to make sure Mom wasn't watching.

"No, I can't—" I started.

He squeezed my arm. "Ten dollars, Goo-Goo. Hurry."

"But—"

"I'll pay you back Monday morning." He raised his right hand. "I swear. Monday morning when I pick you up for school. I'll pay it back. I promise."

I didn't really have a choice. He was squeezing my arm so hard, it was starting to turn red like a salami.

My whole allowance is fifteen dollars. It's supposed to pay for my lunch at school. But I gave Miller two five-dollar bills. "Monday morning, first thing, right?" I said.

He stepped outside and let the screen door slam behind him.

Monday morning after breakfast, Ava met me at my house, and we waited in the front yard for Miller to pick us up. He was always about ten minutes late, and we often had to run to class to get there before the bell. He had a different excuse every morning, but Ava and I knew that none of them were true.

This morning, a car we'd never seen before pulled into my driveway. Squinting into the morning sunlight, I saw Miller behind the wheel. He honked the horn three times even though Ava and I were standing there.

We jogged over to the car. It was a small two-door hatchback, a dull black, not shiny. Peering inside, I saw that the seats were black, too. No color anywhere.

The car definitely wasn't new. The right front fender was bent with a deep gash across it. The door handle was dark from rust. The back window had a small crack in one corner.

Miller rolled a window down. "Hurry. Get in. You're late," he said.

He never apologized. He made it sound like it was *our* fault.

"Whose car is this?" I asked.

"Mine, Goo-Goo," he said, tapping the black steering wheel with both hands.

I pulled open the door. He pulled the seatback forward. "Get in back. Both of you," he said.

"Why?" Ava demanded.

"I'll tell you in a minute. Just get in back."

It was a pretty tight squeeze. The car smelled stale. Like cigarette smoke or maybe food that had been left too long.

Miller shifted into reverse and squealed back down the driveway into the street.

Ava and I were jerked forward, then back. "There aren't any seat belts back here," I said.

Miller didn't reply. He swerved toward the curb as a mail truck rumbled at us.

"How did you get a new car?" Ava asked him.

He gazed at her in the rearview mirror. "I'm going to work part-time at one of my dad's gyms. He bought me this car to go back and forth."

"You're going to start a job?" I said.

"Not really," Miller said. "Dad begged me to fill in. He said he needed someone good. I figure I'll spend most of my time on the machines, working out. I need to keep in shape till I hear what college wants me the most."

Ava and I exchanged glances. We both knew the truth. Miller's dad told him he had to work—or else. I couldn't see his face because we were in the back seat. But I knew his cheeks had to be pink.

"Why do we have to sit in back?" I asked.

The car jerked hard as he stomped on the brakes at a stoplight.

"I wanted to give you a thrill," Miller said.

"Huh? What kind of thrill?" I demanded.

"To sit in a dead man's seat," he said. He squealed through the light. He laughed his dry laugh. "This car is haunted. That's why my dad got it for cheap."

"Haunted? What do you mean?" I said.

"A guy died right where you two are sitting," Miller replied. "He died in the back seat. But his spirit never left the car. He's still in here."

"Give us a break—" I started.

He raised his right hand off the wheel. "I swear. I'm totally serious. He's back there with you. He haunts the car. You're probably sitting on him."

"Miller, give up," Ava said. "We don't believe—"

He kept his right hand raised. "If I'm lying, I'm dying."

I shook my head. "Your dad bought a haunted car?"

"Dad didn't believe the guy who sold it to him. But I believe it. I've had proof."

Some kids from our class waved to us from the sidewalk as we passed by. We were a block from school.

"What kind of proof?" Ava asked.

"Sometimes the car starts up on its own," Miller said. "Sometimes the windows roll down. Last night, the ghost stepped on the gas before I was ready, and I nearly crashed."

Ava and I both burst out laughing. This wasn't the first time Miller tried to scare us. He knew we were both a little scared of ghosts. That's why he made up the story about the dead man in the back seat haunting the car.

"Don't laugh," Miller said. "I'm scared every time I get in the car. I mean, seriously scared. But Dad says I have to drive it."

I saw our school up ahead. Miller slowed the car. "Don't you feel it?" he said, watching us in the rearview mirror. "Feel how cold it is back there? It's ten degrees colder in the back seat. The ghost stays back there, back where he died. Feel something moving around you?"

Miller's voice trembled. I suddenly had the funny feeling that maybe he believed what he was saying. Did he really believe the ghost story? Or was he putting on a good act to scare us?

"Feels fine back here," Ava said. "Nice and cozy."

Miller pulled to the curb in front of our school. I started

to push the seatback in order to climb out. But then I stopped.

"Oh, wait. My ten dollars," I said. "Can I have it?"

Miller turned to look at me. "Ten dollars?"

"You borrowed it on Saturday," I said. "Let me have it, Miller. I need it to buy my lunch."

He squinted at me. "Ten dollars? Why would I borrow ten dollars from you?"

I slapped the seatback angrily. "Just hand it over, okay. You promised."

"No, I didn't," Miller said. "I don't know what you're talking about."

I let out a frustrated sigh. "I'm talking about the ten dollars you said you'd pay back this morning."

He shrugged. "I don't have ten dollars, Goo-Goo." He grabbed the handle and shoved the passenger door open. "Get out of the car. You're going to be late."

For a long time, Ava and I dreamed of paying Miller back for all his lies and all his meanness. But we could never think of a way to have our revenge.

Maybe the money thing was the last straw. I knew Miller never planned to pay back the ten dollars. Now it was definitely time for Ava and me to pay *him* back.

I thought about it all day. And I talked about it with Ava, who had to share her lunch with me since we both had no money. But we couldn't come up with a good plan.

I didn't have an idea until Miller picked us up after school. We stuffed ourselves into the narrow back seat, and Miller turned to us. "I heard whispers back there," he said. "I'm serious. I heard someone whispering, '*I'm here . . . I'm here . . .*'"

"You need a checkup from the neck up," Ava said. It was one of her favorite expressions. I don't know where she heard it.

Miller raised his right hand. "No lie. I heard it plain as day. I almost jumped out of the car." He pulled the car away from the curb. "You're sitting on a ghost. Don't you feel anything?"

We both muttered no.

I didn't have my big idea until Miller dropped us off. He didn't take us home. He parked the car at the curb in front of his house. "I don't feel like taking you the rest of the way," he said. "Why waste my time? You can walk from here."

He climbed out, slammed the driver's door shut, and jogged up the front lawn to his house. "It's starting to rain," Ava said. "Why didn't he take us home?"

I shrugged. "Because he's Miller?"

Ava leaned over the seatback to open the passenger door. "Wait," I said. I pulled her back. "Wait till Miller is in the house. I have an idea."

She dropped back onto the seat. "An idea?"

"To freak Miller out," I said. "Maybe even scare him."

Ava chuckled. "Go ahead. Spill, Paul. What's the plan?"

"We'll make him think there really is a ghost in the car," I said.

"Impossible," she replied.

"Not if we do it slowly," I said. "He'll suspect us at first. But if we keep at it, maybe he'll start to believe . . ."

Ava thought about it. "Okay. I guess we can try," she said. "What do you want to do first?"

The next morning, Miller was in a bad mood when he picked us up for school. "It's a little wet back there," he said as Ava and I climbed into the back seat. "It rained all night. Why did you two leave the windows down?"

"We didn't," I said.

"We didn't touch the windows," Ava added. "Why would we roll down the windows? They were closed when we got out yesterday."

Miller scowled and rolled his eyes. "For sure," he muttered.

"Maybe it was the ghost," I said. "Remember? You told us the ghost rolled down the windows before?"

He didn't answer. He didn't say another word all the way to school.

That afternoon, Miller dropped Ava and me off at my house. He stayed and watched until we were inside. I guess he wanted to make sure we didn't roll down the windows or do something else to the car.

That night after dinner, I told Mom I had a science experiment I had to do. I mixed flour into a big jar of mayonnaise and stirred it all up till it got thick. Then I crept out and hurried to Miller's house.

The car was parked in its usual place at the curb. I checked to make sure no one was watching from the front of the house. Then I pulled open the passenger door, leaned in, and dabbed big globs of my mixture all over the two front seats.

I had a scare when I heard a door slam. I uttered a cry and jerked back from the car. Had I been caught? No. It was a woman in the next house, letting her dog out.

I quietly closed the car door and, gripping the empty mayonnaise jar, made my way home.

The next morning, Miller was twenty minutes late. "Where were you?" Ava and I both demanded.

He muttered something under his breath. "I had to

clean the front seats," he said. "There was white sticky stuff all over them."

"Huh? What was it?" I asked, sounding as innocent as I could.

"At first, I thought birds did it," Miller said. "But there was too much of it. Are you sure it wasn't you?"

"No way," I said. "I was doing a science experiment with Ava last night. I didn't go out."

He eyed the two of us, trying to decide if I was telling the truth.

"Hmmm. White sticky stuff," I said, pretending to think hard about it. I snapped my fingers. "Ectoplasm!" I cried.

He squinted at me. "Huh? Ectoplasm?"

"Ghosts leave ectoplasm wherever they go," I said. "Seriously. You can look it up online."

Miller shook his head. "Ectoplasm," he muttered. "Well . . . why did the ghost leave it on the front seats? Not in back?"

"He probably didn't want to sit in it," Ava answered. A pretty good answer. She's quick.

"No way," Miller murmured. He repeated it all the way to school. "No way . . . No way . . ."

I could see my plan was starting to work. I didn't do anything for the next few days. I wanted to go slow, stretch it out. I had to be careful. I knew Miller would be watching out for Ava and me.

On Saturday, Miller went with his parents on a weekend trip to visit some other cousins in the next town. I knew this was the perfect time for my next move.

I waited till evening to walk to his house. It was a dark night, with low clouds covering the moon and the stars. Gusts of wind made the trees whisper and shake.

His car was parked in its usual place. I wasn't sure what I would do this time—until I saw the keys in the ignition.

What could be more perfect? Miller had left the keys in the car!

I knew exactly what would freak him out. *I'm going to move the car to the next block*, I decided. When he gets home, he'll see that the car isn't where he left it. He'll think the ghost must have moved it.

My heart started to pound as I climbed behind the wheel. I'd never driven a car except at carnival bumper car rides. But how hard could it be to drive one block?

I closed the door and reached for the seat belt. But, of course, the car didn't have seat belts. My hand trembled as I wrapped my fingers around the key and turned it. The car hesitated for a moment, then chugged to life.

I slid my foot from the brake to the gas pedal. My plan was to creep slowly forward to the middle of the next block. There were no other cars on the street. It should be easy.

I gripped the wheel in both hands and started to lower my foot on the gas pedal.

"Hey—!" Something gripped my shoulder from behind.

I opened my mouth in a startled scream.

The car bumped forward, then stopped.

Fingers squeezed into my shoulder. A hand kept me pressed against the seatback. And I heard a harsh whisper in my ears: *"I'm here . . . I'm here . . ."*

"M-Miller? Is that you?" I choked out. "Not funny! You're not funny at all!"

I struggled to turn around. But I couldn't free myself of the tight grasp. Gritting my teeth against the pain, I raised my eyes to the rearview mirror.

And saw . . . nothing.

No one back there.

"I'm here . . ." The hoarse whisper again in my ear.

The hard fingers dug into my shoulder. I took a deep breath—and jerked my body forward. My shoulder slipped from the tight grasp, and I spun around to see who was holding me.

"Huh?" A gasp escaped my throat as I stared into the empty back seat. "Wh-what's happening?" I stuttered, fear choking my throat.

"*I've waited so long . . .*" The whisper tickled my ear like a cold wind. "*It's time. It's time.*"

"The ghost!" I blurted out in a trembling voice. "You're the ghost!"

And then the thought roared through my mind: *Miller told the truth. For once in his life, Miller told the truth!*

I gasped again as the ghost wrapped its hard, bony hands around my neck. The fingers tightened. I struggled to breathe.

"*Waiting . . . I've been waiting,*" came the ghostly whisper. The words sent shivers down my entire body. "*Someone to take my place. I couldn't leave till someone took my place.*"

"Uh . . . uh . . . You mean *me*?" I asked.

"*Goodbye,*" came the cold whisper. "*Goodbye. Thank you for freeing me.*"

Before I could reply, a heavy fog filled the car. Not a white fog. Choking black smoke. It lowered over me like a blanket. I couldn't see. I couldn't breathe.

Darkness. Darkness and a shivering chill.

And then, I opened my eyes and gazed around. I was in the back seat. Floating over the back seat.

Invisible.

I moved my arms. Tested my legs. Invisible and weightless.

I'm light as a cloud.

I gazed out the car window into the night, my mind whirring.

Miller . . . my cousin Miller . . . he had finally told the truth.

He'd be coming soon. He'd be coming to drive his car.

And I had a big decision to make.

Should I congratulate him for finally telling the truth?

Or should I scare him to death?

THE BOY WHO HEARD SCREAMS

I've written lots of stories about kids who see something terrifying or find themselves in horrible trouble. And when they try to get help, no one believes them. They are on their own to face the danger. I think that's a very scary situation.

One day while walking home by myself from middle school, I heard screams coming from an old house on our corner. No one lived there. The house had been empty for as long as I could remember.

But I definitely heard screams coming from a broken upstairs window. I hurried home and told my brother. He didn't believe me. My parents didn't believe me, either. They knew I liked to make up scary stories.

But the screams were real. No one would come with me. But I went back to the house. I gathered my courage and searched inside. I crept through every room, and I didn't find anyone. The house was silent now, silent and empty.

I thought about that house and those screams when I wrote this story.

"HELP! GET HELP!" I CRIED.

I ran into the twins' backyard. Alyssa and Maria were struggling to set up a badminton net. They loved any sport that let them compete against each other. They weren't really that good in sports. They just liked going up against each other and proving who was better.

They dropped the net poles and spun toward me as I came screaming into the yard. Sparky, their dog, started to bark inside the house. Which made me scream louder.

"Hurry! Get help! Hurry!"

"Ted? What's wrong?"

"What's happening?"

They both cried out in alarm. I'll be honest. I can never tell which one is Alyssa and which is Maria. They are real identical twins, and they dress in each other's clothes, and they both have the same short, dark hair. I can't even tell their voices apart.

I was gasping for breath. I'd run all the way from the backyard of the Franco house two blocks away. It was a cool spring day, but my face was drenched in sweat.

"A . . . cat!" I choked out. "I saw a cat!"

"So what? I've seen lots of cats!" That had to be Alyssa. She's the sarcastic one. She's the funny one. Maria is a lot more serious.

"N-no," I stammered. "I saw a cat fall down the old well. In back of the Franco house." I motioned with both hands. "Hurry! Maybe we can pull it out."

I turned and started to run to the street. The girls came trotting after me.

The houses in my new neighborhood are old and big, mostly brick or stone, and the front yards are wide and shady from the many trees. The Franco house is even older, a falling-down mansion that no one has lived in for a hundred years.

"What were you doing at the Franco house?" Alyssa demanded, catching up to me with long, easy strides.

"Just exploring," I said. "I'm from Brooklyn, remember? This neighborhood is like Mars to me."

"You fit in because you're a Martian," she said.

"Not funny!" I cried, my legs pumping harder, my shoes

pounding the grass along the curb. "The cat—it could drown down there!"

We crossed Newton Street and kept running. The Franco house took up most of the next block. The front lawn was overrun with a forest of tall grass and weeds, and the house was buried in shade from the trees that overhung it.

We trampled over old cans and bottles, garbage that someone had left in the gravel driveway, and waded into the backyard. I say *waded* because the weeds were so thick and tall, it felt like we were swimming against a tide of thick water.

Fat evergreen bushes rose up all around us. And some kind of tree brambles formed a fence that we had to dive through to get to the crumbling stone well at the back of the yard.

Alyssa and Maria ran past me. "The well is probably dry," Maria said. "No one has used it in a million years."

"No," I said, breathing hard. "I heard a splash. When the cat fell in, I definitely heard a splash."

They reached the well and gripped the stone sides with their hands.

"I hope we're not too late," I said.

The girls leaned forward and peered down into the old well. I stood a few feet behind them and watched. They both stared hard.

"It's so dark down there," Maria said. "I don't see it."

"No. I don't see it, either," Alyssa said.

I burst out laughing. "Made you look!" I cried.

"Huh?"

"Whoa!"

They both spun toward me, blinking.

"Made you look!" I exclaimed again.

They both put their hands on their waists. "There's no cat?" Alyssa said.

I laughed some more. "No cat."

"Ted, what is your problem?" Maria demanded. Her hands were balled into fists now. "You're such a jerk."

"I made you look," I said. "So, who's the jerk?"

"It isn't funny," Maria said, shaking her head.

"Of course it is," I said. "It's a riot."

I watched them stomp away. Maria tried to shove me as she strode past me, but I dodged out of her reach. They disappeared around the side of the house. I was still chuckling to myself.

Why do I do such wild things?

I guess because I'm bored.

I grew up in Brooklyn in New York City, where it's crowded and noisy and there's always something going on. Somewhere to go. Things to see. Friends to hang out with.

I was never bored back home.

My parents worked at a restaurant in Coney Island. So I got to hang out at the beach, the boardwalk, the amusement park, the aquarium . . . How awesome is that?

But then my parents lost their jobs when the restaurant closed. They didn't know what to do for a while. And then they decided to move here to this tiny town—Hawkins Corners—in the middle of Indiana because my mom has some cousins here.

Hawkins Corners is not Brooklyn.

It's old houses and empty lots and some small soybean farms and a town center one block long with a post office, a gas station, and a diner.

You can understand why I feel like I'm on a different planet. I mean, what am I supposed to do on weekends? Play badminton?

Alyssa and Maria are the only friends I made before school closed for spring break. They said they used to hang out at the mall in Madison Lake, the next town. But most of the stores in the mall closed, and now there's a flea market there in the parking lot. Big whoop.

Mom and Dad work at our cousin's sporting goods store, so I'm on my own a lot. I play *Minecraft* online with my friend JoJo back in Brooklyn. But he's busy a lot, and I don't like to play alone. So I get bored.

And I like to have fun. Sometimes I wish I had a brother or a sister to play jokes on. But since I don't, I guess I'm lucky to have Alyssa and Maria.

A few days ago, I texted Alyssa, and she called me right back. "Ted, what's wrong?"

"Can you come over?" I said. "I locked myself in the basement."

"Huh? How did you do that?"

"I don't know, Alyssa. But I can't get out of the basement, and . . . and there's a huge rat down here."

"A rat?"

"It's as big as a cat. I'm serious. Please, can you come over and let me out?"

"Ted, where are your parents?" Alyssa asked.

"They're at work," I said. I started to sound breathless. I knew Alyssa could hear my panic. "There's no one here. Please come. The kitchen door is unlocked and, and you can get in, and . . ."

There was a long silence. And then Alyssa said, "Oh, I get it. This is one of your silly jokes."

"No. Please," I begged. "Please. It's no joke. The rat— it's staring at me. It's standing up . . . and . . . it's making noises. I . . . I think it's going to attack! I'm really scared. You've *got* to get me out of here."

"Well . . . okay," she said. "Stay up on the basement stairs. Maybe the rat won't climb the stairs. I'll be right over."

I clicked off the phone and ran to my closet. I pulled out my Halloween costume from last year. It's really gross. It's supposed to be Sasquatch, I think, and it has one eyeball hanging out and green drool pouring down the chin.

I think it's a costume for grown-ups. It's too scary for kids. Back in Brooklyn last Halloween, kids pointed at me and stayed away.

I knew it would freak out Alyssa. I pulled the heavy rubber mask over my face. Then I crept into the kitchen broom closet and closed the door behind me.

It was hot and smelled of the cleaning stuff my parents use everywhere. They are total clean freaks and spray and scrub everything in the house. Seriously. The house always smells like a hospital or a doctor's office.

My nose started to burn and my eyes were watering. And the heavy mask made my whole face start to sweat.

Luckily, I didn't have to wait long. A few minutes later, I heard the kitchen door squeak open. I waited a few seconds for Alyssa to step into the house.

I heard the kitchen door close behind her. I knew she was standing right by the broom closet.

One ... two ... three ... four ... GO!

I took a deep breath ... shoved open the closet door ... and burst out, screaming a deafening roar.

Alyssa uttered a gasp. She opened her mouth to scream,

but only a tiny squeak came out. Her hands shot up in the air, and her eyes nearly popped out of her face.

With another terrified squeak, she toppled back, stumbled into the kitchen counter, and dropped to her knees on the floor.

I laughed for twenty minutes. She is so easy to scare.

She climbed to her feet, and her face turned an angry red. She raised both hands and curled them like claws. Then she roared at me and started to punch me with both fists. I was still laughing, and I think that made her even more angry.

I tried to shove her away. But she was determined to punch me. Then she ripped my mask off and heaved it across the kitchen.

"Ted, I can't even—" she said. "How could you?"

"How could *you* fall for my tricks every time?" I said.

"Because I'm a nice person," she said. "Because I really thought you were in trouble."

She scowled at me for a while. I knew she was deciding whether she should punch me some more.

"I'll never believe you again," she said. "I mean it, Ted. Maria and I will never believe you. And . . . we'll find a way to pay you back."

Pay me back? I knew they wouldn't. They weren't like that.

It was spring break. The girls weren't talking to me, and my friend JoJo back in Brooklyn was away with his parents. So I was bored and, yes, lonely.

My dad called me into the den. He was holding the digital camera he had bought me for my birthday. "I have a project for you," he said.

"Mow the front lawn?" I said. That's his usual kind of project.

He shook his head and motioned for me to sit down beside him on the couch. "You like to tell stories, Ted," he said, spinning the camera in his hand. "Why not do a photo essay of that old house you've been hanging around?"

"The Franco house?" I said.

He nodded. "You could take a lot of interesting photos, and put them together to tell a story about the old place. I'll bet Mrs. Fitzgerald would give you extra credit or something."

I gazed at the camera, thinking hard. Maybe Dad had a good idea. I had walked around outside the Franco house several times. But I never thought of photographing it. Maybe I could even go inside.

"Your mom's cousin told me some stories about the

house at the store," Dad said. "Everyone in town thinks it's haunted, of course. Every town has to have a haunted house. But some people have the weird idea that it's in its own time zone. Like the house is stuck in the past or something since no one has lived in it for so many years."

Dad handed me the camera. "That doesn't make any sense," he said. "I don't believe that sci-fi stuff. But I'll bet you could tell an interesting story in photos."

He stared at me, waiting for me to reply.

"Sounds like fun," I said.

I could see the surprise on his face. I usually say no to everything.

It was a gray day with storm clouds high in the sky. A perfect day to start taking photos of the creepy old house. I pulled on my rain slicker, tucked the camera into a pocket, and made my way down the street to the Franco house.

Overgrown hedges nearly blocked the gravel driveway. I pushed through them and gazed over the front yard. A forest of tangled weeds covered the ground beneath low trees that blanketed the entire yard in shadow. The house rose up at the top of the yard like some kind of dark, hulking creature.

Most of the windows were shattered and broken. Maria told me that kids for many generations liked to throw stones at them and knock out the glass.

The Franco house wasn't a house. It was a mansion.

And it was crumbling and falling apart and wrecked in every way.

Shingles were missing and shutters tilted at the windows, and an enormous brown stain covered the front of the tower that loomed over one side of the house.

Most of the slanted roof was bare, and I saw a jagged hole near the top. Some kind of bird had built a huge nest on one of the high window ledges in front of a broken window.

The sky darkened and the air grew cooler as I walked closer to the house. My eyes scanned the tower, the stained front door, the weeds climbing higher than the windows. My mind whirred as I tried to decide what would make the best photos.

I stopped at the bottom of the front stoop and stared at the cracks in the old wooden door.

And that's when I heard the screams.

I froze. At first, I thought it came from far away. It was soft, kind of muffled.

I stood, waiting to hear it again. And yes, another scream. A boy. A long, sad wailing cry.

"Helllllp meeee! Hellllp meeee!"

From inside the house?

"No way," I murmured. "No one has been in there for a hundred years."

"Helllllp meeee! Hellllp meeee!"

My breath caught in my throat. The boy *had* to be in the house. My eyes darted over the broken front windows. I couldn't see him.

A tall hedge stretched over the low windows. I stepped up as close as I could, and I shouted, "Can you hear me?"

No answer.

And then, "Helllllp meeee! Hellllp meeee!" The cry was so shrill and sad and frightened.

"Can't you climb out?" I shouted. "Where are you? Can you come to the window?"

Silence.

I searched the front windows again. Was he in the back? I started to trot to the side of the house when his cry stopped me. "Helllllp meeee! Hellllp meeee!" So close, yet muffled, as if he was shouting through a thick fog.

"I'm right here!" I shouted. "How can I help?" My heart was thudding like a bass drum now, and my head rang with the echo of his shrill cries.

"Helllllp meeee! Hellllp meeee!"

I cupped my hands around my mouth and screamed as loud as I could. "Where are you? Tell me where you are. I will help you."

Silence.

"Can you hear me?" I screamed. "Answer me! Can you hear me?"

Silence.

And then the long, sad wail again: "Helllllp meeee! Hellllp meeee!"

I ran back to the front stoop and climbed the rotting wooden steps. The brass handle on the front door was covered with rust. But I grabbed it and pulled. No. I pushed. No. It was solidly locked.

"Helllllp meeee! Hellllp meeee!" So desperate and sad.

"Okay. I'll get help!" I shouted. I took a deep breath, trying to slow my racing heartbeats. "I'll get help! We can get you out of there."

I grabbed my phone. My hand was trembling. Who could I call? Mom and Dad were at the store. I knew they couldn't come.

My brain was spinning. I couldn't think straight. I couldn't get those frightening screams out of my head.

Almost without realizing it, I punched Alyssa's number. She answered on the third ring. "Ted? What do you want?" She snapped. I knew she was still angry at me.

"There's a boy trapped inside the Franco house," I said breathlessly. "Come help me. We have to get him out."

There was a long silence. And then Alyssa said, "Good one, Ted. Go away."

"No. Please. You've got to believe me. You've got to come help me."

"LOL," she said. "Bye." And she clicked off.

My fingers shook so hard, I could barely tap Maria's number.

She didn't believe me, either.

"It's not a joke. I swear!" I cried.

"*You're* a joke," she said. "Do you seriously think we'll fall for any of your tricks again?"

She clicked off before I could answer.

"I'll be back!" I yelled into the house. "I'll be back and I'll bring help."

I ran home and waited for Mom and Dad to get there. I greeted them as they pulled up in the driveway. They climbed out, surprised to see me standing there. Dad had a big bucket of fried chicken in his hands.

"Hey, Ted," he said. "Let's eat it while it's still hot." He started to the kitchen, but I grabbed his arm.

"We can't," I said. "We have to hurry to the Franco house. There's a boy inside. He keeps screaming for help."

Dad shook his head. "Alyssa and Maria told us about your jokes, Ted. This isn't a good time."

"Save your jokes for your friends," Mom said. "Sid and I worked hard today. We need to sit down and have dinner."

I followed them into the kitchen. Dad set the chicken bucket down on the counter and started to pull plates from the shelf.

"It isn't a joke," I said. "I swear it isn't a joke. The boy is trapped in that old house, and he's screaming—"

"Why didn't you call 911?" Mom demanded. "Why didn't you call the police?"

I swallowed hard. "Oh, wow. I didn't even think of it," I said. "I was so upset and worried, I guess I wasn't thinking clearly."

Dad handed me a plate with two pieces of chicken and mashed potatoes and a biscuit on it. "Go sit down."

"No. You've got to listen," I said. "There is a boy in the Franco house and he needs help."

"Tell you what," Dad said. "Let's have our dinner, and then we'll walk over there and see what we can do."

"That's a plan," Mom said. "After dinner, Ted."

I had no choice. I sat down and stared at my plate. I nibbled at a wing, but I couldn't eat much. I kept hearing those sad, frightened screams.

"Finish your potatoes," Mom said.

"I'm not hungry," I murmured.

"Did you take any photos of the Franco house?" Dad asked.

"I couldn't," I told him. "The boy was screaming and—"

Dad jumped to his feet. "Okay. Let's go over there. If someone is really in trouble . . ."

I raised my right hand. "I swear. A boy is in there, and he's screaming for help."

Mom dropped her napkin to the table and stood up. "If this is one of your jokes, Ted . . ."

"It isn't!" I cried. "I promise. It isn't a joke."

So the three of us walked to the Franco house. It had turned into a warm spring night. Rows of red and yellow tulips had bloomed in our neighbor's front yard. The air felt fresh and sweet.

But I couldn't enjoy it. I knew the boy in the house was frightened and desperate and alone.

The house rose up in front of us like a huge shadow against the gray night sky. I led them up the driveway and to the hedge by the broken front window.

"This is where I heard the screams," I said. "I was standing here and on the front stoop."

The three of us stared into the window. Solid black inside. We listened as we stared. I realized I was gritting my teeth. I took a breath.

We didn't move. I barely breathed. I heard a car roll down the street behind us, music floating out the window. A door slammed somewhere across the street.

Finally, I couldn't wait any longer. I cupped my hands around my mouth and started to shout. "Are you in there? Can you hear me? We came to help you. Can you hear me?"

Silence.

A bird cawed loudly high in a tree near the street.

Silence.

"Hey, are you in there?" I cried. "We came to help you!"

Silence.

Dad took Mom's arm and turned to the driveway. "Let's go, Maureen."

"No. Wait. Please," I said. I jumped in front of them. "Just a little while longer. He's in there. I know it."

Dad pushed his way through the overgrown weeds and stepped onto the front stoop. He grabbed the rusted door handle and tried the door. "The door is jammed shut," he said. "The wood got swollen over time. Ted, there's no one in this house. There hasn't been anyone here in decades."

Mom shook her head. "Ted, what were you thinking? If this was a joke, it isn't funny."

"I swear I heard the screams," I said. "I promise. It wasn't a joke."

Dad sighed and jumped off the stoop. "Let's go home. We didn't finish our dinner. And I brought home a special dessert."

"What is it?" I asked.

"Too special to tell you," he said. He put an arm on my shoulder as we walked to the street. It meant he forgave me for dragging him to the Franco house.

That made me feel better. But I knew what I heard, and I had to know what was going on in that house. I had to go back to the Franco house.

After breakfast the next morning, I grabbed my camera and made my way down the street to the old mansion. It was a cool morning with the sun still a red ball low in the sky. The trees with their new leaves shimmered and shook in a soft breeze.

My shoes crunched up the driveway, and I gazed over the tall grass and weeds to the house. I raised my camera and focused on the huge bird's nest resting on a high window ledge. I clicked the photo—and heard the scream.

"Hellllllp meeee! Hellllp meeee!"

I gasped. The camera slipped out of my hands and hit the grass. I scooped it up and ran closer to the house.

"Helllllp meeee! Hellllp meeee!"

"I'm here!" I shouted. "Where are you? Can you hear me?"

"Helllllp meeee! Hellllp meeee!"

"Can you hear me?" I screamed so loudly my throat throbbed with pain. "Where are you?"

Silence.

He sounded so close. Why didn't he answer?

"Helllllp meeee! Hellllp meeee!" His voice so shrill and terrified.

I moved close to the front window. "I'm coming in," I said. "I'm coming to get you. Don't be afraid."

Silence.

I knew I couldn't get in the front, so I jogged to the back

of the house. I tried the kitchen door, but it was locked and jammed as tight as the front door.

I stepped back and studied the windows. They were all high off the ground, too high for me to climb onto.

"Helllllp meeee! Helllllp meeee!"

I heard the scream clearly back here. I turned and gazed across the yard. "Oh, wow," I muttered to myself when I saw the small wood ladder on its side, nearly covered in weeds.

I pulled it from the weeds and carried it to the kitchen window. The wood was cracked and stained, but the ladder seemed sturdy enough to hold me.

I took a deep breath and climbed up three rungs to the window ledge. The glass was missing. I could see only darkness inside.

With a groan, I hoisted myself off the ladder, onto the ledge. Then I slid through the window and dropped to the floor. It was a deeper drop than I imagined, and pain shocked my knees as I landed.

I took a minute to catch my breath. It had to be at least ten degrees colder inside the house. A sour smell invaded my nose. The air in the kitchen felt heavy and damp.

I waited for my eyes to adjust to the darkness. The kitchen came into focus. I saw broken cabinets with their doors hanging loose. Dark mold covered the front of the old-fashioned stove. A long, cracked kitchen counter was dotted with mouse droppings.

"Ugh." The powerful odor was making me feel queasy. I tasted it in my mouth, thick and bitter. I took short breaths.

I suddenly realized I was shivering. I didn't want to be here. I wanted to climb back outside. But I had to find the frightened boy. His screams repeated in my mind.

"Where are you?" I shouted. My voice echoed off the bare walls. "I'm here. Tell me where you are!"

Silence.

I heard a scuttling sound. Mice running over the floorboards.

I forced myself to move. The front room was cluttered with crumbling, rotting furniture. My shoes scraped through at least an inch of dust.

I sneezed and dust flew in front of my face. My stomach lurched from the heavy odor.

"Where are you?" I screamed. "I'm here! I'm in the house!"

I heard the scuttling sound again. The floorboards creaked. I could see sunlight through the broken front window. But the world seemed far away from this cold, dark place.

My skin prickled. I hadn't expected to be so scared. I stumbled over a rotting cushion on the floor and fell against a couch, sending up a wave of dust.

"Hey, I'm here!" I shouted again. "Please—tell me where to find you."

Silence.

"I heard your screams. I'm here to help you!" My shout rang throughout the enormous house.

I moved from room to room, kicking up dust, trying not to breathe the putrid air. The long dining room table was set, as if guests were expected. But the plates were covered with green mold. A skinny rat stood on the edge of the table, watching me.

I moved down a long hall, peering into bedroom after bedroom. No sign of the screaming boy. Mice scattered as I stepped into a long, empty room. Thick spiderwebs hung from the torn curtains.

Maybe it had been a ballroom, like in the old movies. I peered into the dusty air. The boy wasn't there.

How long did I search? Maybe an hour. There were so many rooms. So many empty rooms.

I have to get out of here, I told myself finally. *I can't breathe. I'm covered in dust. I'll never get this sour odor out of my nose and mouth.*

Somehow, I found my way back to the front room. I stepped up to the door and grabbed the handle.

"Oh, wow!" I let out a cry as it came off in my hand.

I stood there staring at the brass handle. I tried to push it back into the door, but it kept sliding right out.

Angrily, I tossed the handle to the floor and strode quickly to the kitchen. My heart pounding, I grabbed the lock in the back door and clicked it open. I pulled on the handle . . . pulled . . . The door wouldn't budge.

I tried pushing it. Then I tugged the handle with both hands. The door was jammed shut.

"Okay, okay," I said aloud. "Stay calm, Ted. You can get out of here. Easy."

The windows. The glass was missing in many of them. I gazed at the window I had used to climb in. Too high. I needed the ladder that stood outside.

No ladder. No ladder in the house.

And the windows so high. All of them too high.

I felt myself losing it.

The dust . . . the creeping green mold . . . the herds of mice . . . the smell . . . the horrible smell . . .

I raised my face to the kitchen window and screamed:

"Hellllllp meeee! Hellllp meeee!"

There had to be someone outside. Someone nearby. Someone who could get me out of this frightening old house.

"Hellllllp meeee! Hellllp meeee!"

Would anyone hear my screams?

I ran from room to room. Frantic. My throat choked in panic. My skin tingling.

The windows all so high. The doors jammed.

"Helllllp meeee! Hellllp meeee!"

And yes, I realized it. How could I not realize it?

I was the screaming boy.

I was the boy I heard screaming inside the house.

Sure, I'd read stories about people and places trapped in time, trapped in a different reality. And I'd seen scary movies about people caught in a time warp, unable to get back in the real world.

But I never expected to be living it!

Suddenly, I knew. The house was locked in time. In its own time zone.

And standing outside, I had been hearing *myself*, *my* screams, *my* terror.

"Helllllp meeee! Hellllp meeee!"

There's no one out there. No one to hear. But I had to try.

And then . . . wait.

A thought made me freeze.

My phone. I had my phone. I jerked it from my jeans pocket.

"Yes!" I screamed out loud. "Yes!"

Would it work? Did I have bars? Could I call for help?

"Yes!"

My parents were at the store. I didn't want them to know the trouble I'd gotten myself into. I didn't want them to know. Maria was away at her aunt's house.

Alyssa. It had to be Alyssa.

My hand shook so hard, I could barely punch in her number.

Please answer. Please answer.

No. It went to voice mail. Okay . . . That's okay . . .

I took a breath and left a frantic message: "Alyssa, I need your help. I'm trapped inside the Franco house. Please come and help get me out. Please hurry!"

I tucked the phone back into my pocket and let out a long whoosh of air.

She'll come. I know she'll come.

Why wouldn't she come?

BUGS

When people are asked, "What are you afraid of?" spiders are always at the top of the list. Lots of scary stories have been written about attacks by spiders and other insects. Bees are scary. So are wasps and hornets. Horror movies have even been made about ordinary houseflies.

This summer, I found stink bugs in my house. Talk about scary and nasty!

It made me start to think about bugs . . . Maybe I could write a story about all kinds of bugs. Maybe I could write about a boy who was scared of all bugs.

Alvie, in this story, is terrified of even the thought of bugs. And guess what. He has good reason to be afraid.

You might want to read this story with a can of bug spray nearby.

"KILL IT! KILL IT!" I SCREAMED.

Dad looked up from the iPad on his lap. "What?"

David laughed.

"KILL IT! PLEASE!" I jumped off the couch and staggered back, stumbling over the shag rug.

Dad stood up and set the iPad down. He took a few slow steps toward me, as if it wasn't an emergency.

My brother David had the usual grin on his face. Like he was better than me because he wasn't afraid. "Alvie, what is it?" he asked. "A flea?"

"No! Bigger!" I cried. "See it? On the arm of the couch."

David laughed again. "A fly. It's just a fly."

Dad shook his head. "Don't say it's just a fly, David. You know Alvie has a problem. Try to be serious."

"Why don't we just stand here and discuss it?" I cried. I shuddered. "I can hear it *buzzing*. DO something!"

"I'll open the front window and maybe it will fly out," Dad said. He works for the fire department, and he's always interested in saving lives.

I let out a cry as the fly darted off the couch and buzzed around my head. I could feel the wind off its wings. "No! Kill it! It's attacking me!" I slapped my hand back and forth in the air, trying to brush it away.

David's dark eyes flashed, and his grin grew wider. He shrugged. "You can't kill it. I hid the flyswatter," he said.

Dad scowled at him. "You couldn't be that cruel," he said. "A joke is a joke, but—"

"Just messing with you," David said. He reached under the side table and pulled the flyswatter up from its usual place. My parents keep a swatter in each room—even in the bathrooms—in case I have a bug emergency.

David leaned over the back of the couch. He slowly raised the swatter over his head, and—SLAM—smacked the leather with it.

"Got it!" he cried.

"No, you didn't," I said. My heart was pounding. Arms crossed tightly in front of me, I took a few more steps back across the den. "You just swatted the couch. The fly wasn't even there."

"No. I killed it," David insisted. "I have fast reflexes. That's why I can hit a baseball, and you can't."

I squinted at the couch cushion. "If you killed it, where is it?"

"That's enough," Dad said. He took the swatter from David. Dad doesn't like arguing. "I don't see any flies now. So, just drop it."

"Drop what?" Mom asked, walking into the den. She had a pile of catalogs in her arms. Mom works at a baby clothes store downtown. She spends hours looking at photos of baby clothes.

"Alvie saw a fly," David said.

I really did want to wipe the grin off his face. But I think it's permanently glued on.

"I didn't *see* a fly," I said. "I was *attacked* by a fly."

Mom turned to Dad. "I thought you were discussing sleepaway camp with them."

Dad waved the iPad in front of him. "I was looking up sleepaway camps, but—"

"I can't go!" I said. "No way! You *know* I can't go. Too many bugs!" I shuddered again.

"I wasn't looking for you, Alvie," Dad said. "David wants to be a junior counselor this summer. I was looking up camps for him."

I let out a long whoosh of air. "Okay. You scared me."

I turned and saw Mom studying me. "We're going to deal with your problem," she said, just above a whisper.

"I don't have a problem," I told her. "I just don't like bugs."

And I think bugs *know* that I don't like them. And so they attack me a lot more than most people. Bugs climb into my shoes, and land on my head, and climb up my leg, and bite the back of my neck, and fly up my nose, and follow me everywhere I go.

I almost swallowed a bug once. I could taste it on my tongue for weeks.

So, there was no way I could go to sleepaway camp. It made my skin itch just to think about it.

That night, I went upstairs to my room. I knew what the squeaking sound was before I even turned on the light. It was Happy, my hamster, going for his nightly run on the wheel in his cage.

"Have a good workout, Happy," I said. Then I clicked on the ceiling light—and screamed in horror.

"SPIDER! A GIANT SPIDER!"

The ugly black creature clung to my pillow.

I grabbed my throat. It ached from my scream.

David came bursting out of my closet, laughing like a lunatic. "It worked!" he cried, raising both fists in triumph. "It worked!"

He grabbed the spider between his fingers and squeezed it. "Rubber," he said. "Alvie, you fell for a rubber spider."

"It . . . it looks very real," I choked out.

"Real?" He tossed it at me. It bounced off my chest and dropped to the floor. "It's bigger than a lemon," he said. "How could it be real?"

"Why?" I asked, my throat still throbbing. "Why did you do it?"

He shrugged. "What are brothers for?"

"Another bug joke, David?" Dad stood in the bedroom doorway. "How many times do I have to tell you? We can't joke. Alvie has a serious problem."

Which is how I ended up in Dr. Hirsch's office.

"Come in and sit down, Alvie," she said. She motioned to a small armchair across from her desk. Dr. Hirsch was younger than I had imagined, younger than my parents. She spoke in a soft, whispery voice and had a nice smile.

Mom stayed at the office door. "As I explained over the phone," she said, "Alvie is not a frightened kid. He is normal in every way. He just has this one phobia—bugs."

"Well then, Alvie and I will have a nice talk about bugs and how scary they are," the doctor said.

Mom backed out and closed the door behind her. Dr. Hirsch sat down behind her desk and moved some papers around. She picked up glasses with round red frames and slid them onto her nose. Then she raised her eyes to me.

"Alvie, where shall we start?" she asked. "Do you think you are more scared of bugs than most other people?"

I thought about it for a moment. "I think I'm the *right amount* of scared," I answered.

That made her chuckle. "Good answer," she said. She pushed the glasses up on her nose. "Think back. Think really hard. Can you remember the first time you were frightened by bugs?"

I slid back in the chair and crossed my arms in front of me. "The first time?"

She nodded. "Do you remember anything when you were really young?"

"Well . . ." I thought hard. "Yes. It was a picnic. In the park. Mom and Dad and my big brother, David. And some other people. I guess they were my cousins. I was really little . . ."

Dr. Hirsch leaned forward over the desk. "And what happened?"

"I . . . uh . . . I picked up a peanut butter sandwich," I said, picturing it in my mind. "And there was an ant crawling on the bread. A black ant. I remember I started to cry. I started to cry and I couldn't stop."

Dr. Hirsch nodded. Her eyes were locked on mine. I could see she was thinking hard.

"Ants are very tiny," she said. "We have to figure out

why you were so afraid of something that small. Tell me, were you ever stung by a bee?"

I shivered. "No. Never. But when you said that, it made my stomach hurt."

"How about mosquito bites?" she asked. "Do you get a lot of mosquito bites?"

I shook my head. "Not really."

"Alvie, do kids in your class at school know about your fear of bugs? Do any of them make fun of you?"

"My brother, David, makes fun of me all the time," I told her. "He thinks it's a big joke."

She sat back in her chair. She twisted a finger through a strand of her black hair. "Well, you and I know it isn't a joke," she said. "And how about kids at school?"

"Well . . ." I thought hard. "I was in class one day at the beginning of the school year, and I felt a bug crawling up my leg." Thinking about it, my leg started to itch.

"What did you do?" the doctor asked.

"I jumped to my feet, and I started to scream," I said. "Mrs. Ridley, my teacher, ran over and pulled up my pants leg. And . . . and she pulled a ladybug off my leg."

Dr. Hirsch blinked. "Really? A ladybug?"

"Yes. A tiny red ladybug. She held it up for the class to see, and everyone went nuts because I had screamed like that."

"That must have been very embarrassing for you," Dr. Hirsch said.

A bell dinged on her cell phone on the corner of her desk.

"Our time is up for today," she said. "But you and I should keep talking. Do you want to?"

"I guess," I said.

She stood up. "I think if we keep talking and remembering things, we can get to the bottom of your bug problem. You'd like that, wouldn't you?"

I nodded. "Sure." She led me to the door.

Mom was sitting in the waiting room. She looked up from her phone as we came out.

"Alvie and I had a good talk," Dr. Hirsch told her. "He wants to come back. I think we'll figure things out."

I waited by the front door as they chatted for another minute or two. I didn't hear what they were saying. I kept thinking about that picnic when I was little, and the ant crawling on my sandwich.

"She seems very nice," Mom said as we drove home. "Did you like her?"

I nodded. "Yes. She was okay. She didn't seem like a doctor. More like a person."

That made Mom smile. "You know, it's almost your birthday, Alvie. Have you thought about what birthday present you would like?"

I didn't have to think about it. I already knew what I wanted. "I'd like a bug zapper," I said. "To put out on the patio. Then I could sit out there and the bugs wouldn't bother me."

Mom pressed her lips together tightly. "Think of something else," she said. "Okay? Think of something a little more fun."

The piñata was Dad's idea.

He brought home a big rainbow-colored piñata, shaped like a bull with two short horns on its head, a fat belly, and a fierce expression on its face. "It's packed with candy and toys," he said. "Your friends at your birthday party will love it."

"Where are you going to hang it?" I asked.

"On the tree branch that hangs over the patio," he said. "I'm going to hang it really high. You can swat at it with a broom handle."

David took the piñata from Dad and held it in front of him. "Can we take a peek inside?" he asked. "I want to see what candy to grab."

"Of *course* you can't," Dad said. "You'll wreck it."

David sighed and tossed the piñata at me. It nearly knocked me over. "Hey, it's heavy!" I cried.

"It's going to be an awesome party," Mom said.

Ever since I had that visit with Dr. Hirsch, everyone was being nice to me. Even David. He stopped putting rubber insects in my bed. He didn't even tease me when I screamed at a big spider in the driveway and it turned out to be a clump of dirt.

David and I held the ladder for Dad as he worked to string the piñata over the tree branch. It turned out to be a waste of time, because it rained on the day of my party. We had to move everything inside.

Our living room has a long wooden rafter up along the ceiling. And that's where Dad hung the big paper bull. "When you swing the broom handle at it, you'll have to be careful not to knock over my lamps," Mom warned.

Mom has these two tall dragon lamps from China. She shows them off to everyone who comes to the house.

"I'll be blindfolded," I reminded her. "But I'll try to be careful."

The rain was beating down when kids started to arrive. We had a big pile of wet coats and raincoats on the bench beside the front door. There are eighteen kids in my class. They all came except for Aaron Stengel and Ashley Hopper, who were sick.

So, the living room was jammed with kids. There wasn't much room to move around, and it got pretty steamy in the room. I mean damp and hot and sweaty. But we had good music going, and good pizza and other snacks. And I think kids were having a good time.

Of course, everyone kept looking up at the big paper bull hanging above us. And after we all had cake, David took the broom and swatted the handle at it, sending the piñata swinging from side to side.

Dad grabbed the broom away from him and handed it to me. "Guess it's time to open the piñata," he announced. "What do you think is inside it?"

Everyone shouted their ideas at once. We all knew it was candy and small toys. Mom had one of Dad's neckties that she wrapped around my eyes as a blindfold. She moved me through the crowd of kids to the center of the room.

"Okay, birthday boy. Swing away!" Dad said.

I knew the piñata was right above me. But in the darkness behind the blindfold, I felt confused, sort of off-balance.

I raised the broomstick and swung it hard.

Missed.

Kids laughed.

I turned a little and swung again. The broomstick whooshed through the air.

"Careful of my lamps!" Mom cried.

Gazing into the solid black, I concentrated. I twirled the handle in my hands, then swung hard with all my might.

I heard a *craaack*. And felt a hard *thump*.

Yes! I smacked the bull. I heard it break open. I felt soft taps on my shoulders and the top of my head. Stuff was coming down.

I gasped as I heard screams all around me. Not happy screams. Screams of horror. Alarmed cries and kids shrieking and crying, "No! No! No!"

I ripped the blindfold off my face and blinked my eyes. I seemed to be standing in a black rain falling from the open piñata. *Black rain?*

All around me, kids were ducking their heads, trying to cover themselves with both hands, staggering and stumbling. "Bugs!" a girl screamed. "Bugs!"

And I finally realized. *Hundreds* of bugs were raining down on everyone, pouring down from the hole in the piñata. A storm of fat black bugs.

I batted them off my shoulders. I swiped my hand over my head, sending bugs toppling to the floor. I pulled them off the front of my shirt.

"Noooooooo!"

"Helllllp!"

Cries of horror rang off the walls. Kids were running in all directions. I started to walk, and the fat bugs cracked and squished under my shoes. Bugs swarmed over the living room carpet. I saw dozens of them climbing the walls.

Gasping for breath, I even saw bugs slithering up my mom's Chinese lamps!

Covering their heads, kids stumbled toward the back hall and the kitchen. I slapped a bunch of the fat insects off my neck. "Noooo!" A cry burst from my throat as I felt the pinch of bugs on my legs.

"Noooo! Nooo!" I slapped at them as I ran.

I glanced up and saw that the storm of bugs hadn't stopped. They were still pouring down. Coming down hard and bouncing off the carpet, off the tables and the couch.

I saw David on his back on the floor, swarmed over by bugs. A blanket of bugs!

Mom huddled against the wall, her hands covering her face. I glimpsed Dad holding up coats at the front door. "Let's get out of here, everyone!" he shouted. "Let's get you all to safety."

I didn't wait to get my coat. I burst out the front door into the rain. I had to get the feel of the bugs off my skin. My whole body tingled, and I itched so hard, I could barely walk.

I raised my face to the cold rain and let it wash over me.

I turned and saw kids running from the house, their coats and raincoats open. Some of them were still slapping bugs off their heads and swiping them out of their hair. Their screams drowned out the whoosh of the rain.

David came running up to me, his shoes splashing up

rainwater in the grass. "Alvie—are you okay?" he cried. "Are you—" Then he stopped and his eyes went wide. He reached up a hand—and pulled a fat bug from his nose.

He squashed it in his hand and wiped his hand on the leg of his jeans. "Don't freak out, Alvie," he said. "Try to stay calm, okay? It will all be okay. Dad says he'll call an exterminator."

I couldn't go back in the house. None of us could.

We spent the rest of my birthday in a tiny damp room at the Shady Rest Motel across town. I couldn't stop scratching. My skin itched so much even though the bugs were gone. My hair tingled, as if bugs were still crawling through it.

Mom kept shaking her head and muttering to herself. David sat on the floor and put a hockey game on the TV. He was scratching, too.

Dad sat on the edge of a bed with the phone pressed to his ear. "I found an exterminator who can come tomorrow," he said.

"Did you reach the party store that sold you the piñata?" Mom asked.

Dad frowned and shook his head. "I called three times. No one answered."

"How could that happen?" I said. "How could they have a piñata full of bugs?"

"That's what I want to know!" Dad said.

"Happy birthday, Alvie," David said. Then he burst out laughing.

Two days later, we moved back into the house. "Whoa! The smell—it's gross!" I cried. I pinched my nose shut. My eyes started to water.

"They must have sprayed every inch," Dad said. "I'm sure we are bug-free now."

"I think we should move," I said. They thought I was joking, but I wasn't.

I couldn't help it. I tried to calm down, but I kept imagining bugs everywhere I looked. The odor made my nose and eyes burn. Sitting in the den, I stared at the rug, searching for little crawly things.

Every time I shut my eyes, I saw the piñata again, cracked open and spewing the shower of fat black bugs down over all my friends.

"What are you thinking about, Alvie?" Mom asked.

"Guess," I said.

I decided to go up to my room and do some homework. Maybe that would take my mind off bugs, at least for a short while.

As I stepped into my room, I heard the squeaking hamster wheel. *Happy must be going for another run*, I thought.

I peered into the cage—and my breath caught in my throat.

"Nooooo."

Happy wasn't on the wheel. A shiny, six-legged bug—as round as a tennis ball—ran on the wheel!

"Ohhhhh." I felt my stomach lurch. "Happy? Where are you?"

I peered into the glass cage. No sign of the hamster. Two enormous bugs crawled through the sawdust on the cage floor. The bug on the wheel picked up speed, making it squeak even louder.

I covered my ears and screamed, "Mom! Dad! Come quick!"

I heard footsteps hurrying up the stairs. "Alvie? What's wrong?" David called.

He burst into my room.

I pointed to the hamster cage. "Look—" But I stopped with a gasp.

David's face—it was all wrong. I blinked, trying to see him correctly. But I couldn't blink away the two antennae poking up from the top of his head. The stubby black fur that covered his face. The glassy eyes that rose above jagged insect teeth.

David clicked two sharp pincers in the air.

"Noooo!" I shrieked. "Get away! Get out of my room! You . . . you're not David! You're a bug. You—"

I ducked my head low and shoved him out of the way. I raced down the hall and then down the stairs, screaming all the way. "Mom! Dad! Where *are* you? Help! Please!"

I stumbled to a stop in the living room. My screams caught in my throat as I saw them.

Mom and Dad were hanging upside down from the ceiling. They had stick legs, like flies. Their narrow wings fluttered at the sides of their sleek, black insect bodies. Antennae on the tops of their heads waved down at me.

"Noooooo!" A shrill moan escaped my throat, and I dropped to my knees, shuddering in horror. "What is happening?" I wailed. "Tell me! Please—tell me! How can this be happening?"

They let go of the ceiling and fluttered down toward me, their wings buzzing. They circled me, whirring close to my face, pincers snapping at me.

"Alvie," Dad buzzed. "Don't you know? Don't you know what is happening?"

"Come in, Alvie," Dr. Hirsch said in her whispery voice. She motioned toward the armchair across from her desk. "Have a seat, and let's talk."

"Yes," I said. "Talk. I—I—" I couldn't find the words. I didn't know where to start.

She lowered herself behind the desk and removed her glasses. "Take a deep breath, okay? Just take a long, slow breath, and then let it out. You've got to calm down."

"Calm down? How can I?" I cried. "Bugs everywhere. My brother. My parents!"

She motioned me down with both hands. "Ssshhhh. Deep breath," she said. "Alvie, I think you are forgetting some things."

I blinked. "Huh? Forgetting?"

She nodded. "I think you are forgetting that you're not real."

I blinked again. I opened my mouth to reply. But what could I say to that?

"Think hard, Alvie," the doctor said. "Try to remember. You're not a real boy. You are a character in a horror movie."

I stared back at her, waiting for her words to make sense.

"You have the starring role, Alvie," she continued. "You are the lead in a horror movie. You are a character in the movie. You're not real."

"I—I'm *not*?" I stammered.

"You are the star of *Bugs II*," she said. "And everyone is expecting the sequel to do even better than the first movie. Don't you remember? You got the part because you really are afraid of insects—and because you have a great scream of horror. Your scream was better than any of the other actors."

I thought hard. "I'm starting to remember," I said.

"That's better," Dr. Hirsch said. She nodded. And as she nodded, she started to change.

Spiky black hair poked up all around her face. Jagged yellow teeth slid out from her mouth. Her eyes bulged, and thin wings fluttered up on her shoulders. A sharp stinger shot out from her nose.

Buzzing loudly, she started to float up from her chair.

I jumped to my feet. I stared at her in horror—and started to scream.

HOW TO CHANGE YOUR LIFE

Can a book really change your life?

Yes. A book changed my life when I was ten years old. It was a book of short stories by the sci-fi author Ray Bradbury. Before I discovered it, I wasn't a book reader. I read only comic books.

One summer day, a librarian greeted me at the door to the library. "Bob," she said, "I know you like comic books. Here's something else you will like." She led me to the shelf of Ray Bradbury stories.

She was right. I loved the short story book so much, I wanted to read more, more, more. The book changed my life by turning me into a reader.

Here's a story about a boy who also finds a book that changes his life. But his story is not like mine!

MY NAME IS MUNROE LACKWITZ AND I HATE MY LIFE.

I'm not an unhappy person. I think I'd be a *very* happy person if I had a different life.

Right now, I'm buried up to my head in burning hot sand. That's because I fell asleep on the beach, and my friends, Fiona and Devin, piled a ton of sand over me and packed it so tight I can't move.

I call Fiona and Devin my friends, but that's only if you think friends are people who like to embarrass you and make fun of you and play tricks on you and get you into endless trouble.

Different friends would change my life. But I don't have different friends. I have Fiona and Devin.

One of the nice things about living in a beach community like Sandy Harbor is hanging out on the beach with your friends. But not when you are buried up to your head in the sand, and your friends seem to have left you and gone home.

I can't move my head much. But as far as I can see, there's no one else on the beach. The sun is still high in the sky, and it feels like my face is on fire, so I must look like a well-done roast beef.

The sunburn is bad enough. But I'm pretty sure the reason my skin is itchy is because there is a herd of tiny sand crabs crawling up my face. Of course, I can't scratch or brush them away.

Which is another reason to hate my life.

This is bad. But I have to admit that it isn't as bad as last week when Fiona and Devin set fire to my dog.

They didn't mean to set fire to Frankie. I was showing them the new digital fire extinguisher my dad bought because he's a safety freak. And they thought it would be funny to set Frankie's backyard doghouse on fire to test the new device.

They didn't know Frankie was in his doghouse. Fiona and Devin aren't animal killers. They're just irresponsible jerks.

Frankie came running out of his house with only minor tail burns. The new fire extinguisher didn't work, and the doghouse burned to the ground. Mom blamed me for the whole thing because she blames me for everything Fiona and Devin do.

She even blamed me for the shoplifting problem at Seckel's, which wasn't my fault at all. Fiona and Devin thought it would be a riot to have me branded as a shoplifter for life, and maybe get a few free candy bars at the same time.

Believe me, I've never stolen a thing in my life, unless you count the doughnut I took from a display table at the Stop 'n' Shop supermarket. But I was only two and didn't know any better.

Seckel's is a candy store across from the ocean where my so-called friends and I go to buy bags of chips and water bottles to take to the beach.

Mr. Seckel knows my parents, and sometimes he goes bike riding along the coast with my dad. So I would never steal anything from his store, not even a paper napkin. Seriously.

That's why I was so surprised and confused when he stopped me as we were leaving the store with our bags of tortilla chips and water bottles.

Mr. Seckel stepped in front of the door and pointed to my gray hoodie. "What's in your pocket, Munroe?" His eyes were narrowed, and he wasn't smiling.

"My p-pocket?" I stammered. "Nothing. It's empty."

He kept staring at the hoodie. "Want to show me?"

"Sure. No problem." Fiona and Devin had moved back. Fiona stared at the floor. Devin's face was red.

I reached into the deep pocket in the front of my hoodie and gasped when I felt something inside it. My hand started to shake as I pulled out three candy bars. I stared at them in amazement, as if I'd never seen a candy bar in my life.

"How did those get in there?" I blurted out.

"That's what *I* would like to know," Mr. Seckel said, and he sounded angry.

I knew how they got into my pocket. Fiona and Devin were gazing around the store, looking everywhere but at me. They both looked totally guilty, and I knew they *were* guilty.

"I . . . I can pay for them," I choked out. I reached into the back pocket of my shorts for the folded-up money I'd tucked there.

"You *bet you will!*" Mr. Seckel said. He shook his head. "Your family would be very disappointed in you, Munroe."

I handed him four wrinkled-up dollars bills, and we hurried out of the store. As soon as we crossed the parking lot, Fiona and Devin burst out laughing.

"Why did you do that?" I demanded. "Why did you do that to me?"

"We didn't think he'd stop you," Devin said.

"Guess we were wrong," Fiona added.

They thought it was a hoot, but it wasn't. Of course,

Mr. Seckel told my dad about it. And now my parents look at me different, like I'm the family criminal.

Even Buddy, my big brother, who doesn't have an honest bone in his body and has never told the truth in his life, calls me "The Gangster." And he doesn't mean it as a compliment.

Don't get me started about Buddy. Trust me, he's no buddy of mine.

His idea of being a good brother is to bump me against the wall every time he passes by. He gives me about ten hard chest bumps a day. He says he's just being friendly. But since Buddy is twice as big as me, my body is bruised and battered from head to foot.

Even our dog, Frankie, gives me a hard time. Frankie likes to chew on my ankles when I sit at the dinner table. Of course, Mom and Dad say it's my fault. They say I shouldn't hold my ankles so close to Frankie.

But wait. I think I see my brother walking along the beach. Did he come looking for me?

"Hey, Buddy! Buddy!" I try to shout, but my throat is too dry, and the words come out in a hoarse whisper.

But yes, it's my big brother, and he stops in front of me and bends over to peer at my head. "Help . . ." I squeak.

He squints down at me. His wide body is casting a shadow over me. "Is that you, Gangster?" He grins that ugly grin of his. "I thought someone left a shrunken head on the beach."

"Get . . . me . . . out . . ." I beg, my throat aching. "Please . . . dig me out."

"You're getting a bad burn," Buddy says. He tsk-tsked and shook his head. "A seriously bad sunburn."

"Help me . . ." I begged.

"Can't have my little bro all sunburned," he said. He tugged the blue baseball cap off his head. Then he reached down and shoved the cap down onto my head. "There. Much better. Give you a little shade."

His red flip-flops kicked up sand as he started to walk away.

"No . . . please . . ." I begged. "Come back, Buddy. Dig me out of here."

He turned and gave me a two-fingered salute. "Later, dude," he said, and strode on across the beach, kicking up sand as he went.

I let out an angry growl, like some kind of animal. I felt so angry, it gave me new strength. I twisted my body one way, then the other, harder . . . harder . . . until I shook loose the sand around me. Then I pulled myself up and out of the hole.

The hot sand stuck to my skin because my body was drenched with sweat. I touched my face. My sunburned cheek hurt so much, I instantly jerked my hand away.

"Free," I murmured. "I'm free!" Like it was something to celebrate.

I still wasn't free from my miserable life.

I still had to go on living a life I hated.

That didn't change for another week.

A week later, I walked into the Sandy Harbor library. It's a small stone building across from the town hall. It's always peaceful and cool, and I like the creaking sound the old floorboards make when I walk on them. So, okay, I'm weird.

I always take a book or two to the beach. That way, I have something to do when I don't want to talk to Fiona and Devin anymore. I like to read books about other people's lives. Guess why.

Hannah Green, one of the librarians, greeted me from the front desk as I walked in. "Munroe, why is your face peeling?" she asked.

I rolled my eyes. "Thanks for mentioning it," I said. "I had a bad sunburn."

"Looks like you had a *good* sunburn," she said. "Your face is so puckered up. I thought maybe your head was turning into a prune!" She laughed. She thinks she's hilarious.

I gazed around, checking out the long rows of bookshelves. A narrow shaft of sunlight beamed down from the skylight overhead. It made the dust in the air glitter like silver. "No one else here?"

She shook her head. "It's too nice a day. Everyone is at the beach. Why aren't you at the beach?"

"I'm waiting for my face to unpucker," I said. "Also, my friends are at the beach, and I don't really feel like seeing them."

"What's wrong with your friends?" she asked.

"I hate them," I said.

Her mouth dropped open in surprise. "Oh. Wow."

I turned and walked down a narrow aisle between tall shelves. I always started at the biography section to see if any new ones had come in. The section was at the very back of the library, past sports books and science fiction.

I stopped halfway there and gazed up. I thought I heard a swarm of insects. But one of the long ceiling lights was buzzing. The lightbulb flickered, making the books down below appear to be moving.

I stepped up to the biography shelves and began pawing through some books on the middle shelf. I didn't see anything new. I picked up a book with a bright pink cover and the face of a smiling girl on it. She wasn't much older than me.

The book was called *Welcome to My Life*. It was by Devra Carter. I turned it over and read the back cover. It said Devra Carter is sixteen and has three million followers on TikTok.

"Whoa," I muttered to myself. "Devra Carter is sixteen, and she has already published her life story!"

Now, that girl was having an *awesome* life!

I shoved the book back onto the shelf. I didn't want to read about Devra's life. I knew I'd be too jealous.

Something fell onto the floor in front of me. I had bumped another book off the shelf. I bent down and picked it up. It was a small, thin paperback, not many pages.

The book had a white cover with bold black words across the front: *You Can Change Your Life*.

I didn't see an author's name. I turned it around and read the back cover: *Want to change your life? It's easy. Read this book.*

That's all it said.

"This book is on the wrong shelf," I told myself. "It doesn't belong in biography."

I flipped through the pages. "How can a book change your life?"

I dropped down to the floor, sat cross-legged, and

started to skim the book. It was very short. There weren't any chapters or even long paragraphs. It seemed to be a list of things to do.

I started at the beginning. *Think clear thoughts.* That's what it said on page one.

"What does that mean?" I asked myself. "How is that helpful?"

The ceiling light buzzed above me, and the book went in and out of shadow. I read the next page: *Try out a new smile.*

"Total garbage," I muttered. "Who published this? Why would anyone think this is useful?"

I flipped quickly through the next pages: *Walk with a proud stride . . . New clothes can mean a lot . . . Do something with your hair . . .*

I climbed to my feet. The flickering light was starting to get to me. I was about to shove the book back onto the shelf. But I turned to the last page and read it quickly:

Are you ready to change your life?

Read these words out loud—and best of luck to you.

The words were in solid black type. I'd never seen any of them before. Squinting into the shadowy light, I read them out loud.

"Glawson . . . Parkwallaby . . . Monostartic . . . Groostic . . . Maladonia . . . Freepnovia."

"What a joke," I muttered to myself. I tossed the book

onto the shelf and made my way to the front of the library. Hannah Green wasn't at the front desk, so I walked out without saying goodbye to her.

Blinking in the bright afternoon sunlight, I stepped down the library steps and waited on the sidewalk for my eyes to adjust. "There you are!" a voice called.

A woman in a white tennis outfit, her blond hair flying behind her, came running toward me. "Jonah, you said you'd only be a few minutes," she said breathlessly. "I've been waiting all this time. You're going to be late for the theater."

"Huh?" I swallowed. "Jonah? I'm sorry, but—"

She grabbed my arm and tugged. "Hurry. The limo is around the corner. There's a crowd waiting."

"I'm not Jonah," I said, pulling back. "You're making a mistake."

She swung a white pocketbook around, tugged it open, and pulled out a hand mirror. "We have to do something about your hair. You can't show up looking like this."

She raised the mirror to my face—and I gasped.

It wasn't my face!

I stared at coppery hair, shaved close on one side of my head . . . green eyes . . . a silvery ring in one ear . . . a dimple in one cheek . . .

I wasn't even sunburned!

"That's not me!" I cried. "That's not my face!"

The woman pulled a hairbrush from the pocketbook. "Hush. Stop it. Listen to me, Jonah. I'm your mother. I wouldn't lie to you. Sure, we're in a small town. But the press conference is important. Stand still. Let me brush your hair."

"Don't you see? I'm not Jonah," I choked out. "You're not my mother."

"Stop mumbling," she snapped. She squeezed my shoulder and scraped the brush down the side of my hair.

What was I wearing?

A tight blue T-shirt with a red leather vest over it? Black denim pants ripped at both knees.

Not my clothes! Not what I was wearing when I went into the library.

The library. Slowly . . . slowly it was dawning on me what had happened. That book . . . those made-up words . . .

It really *did* change my life!

Here is what I learned in the limo in the ride to the Lyceum movie theater in the next town. My name is Jonah Quicken, and I was the lead singer in a boy band called Hoodie Brothers. I left the band to be in movies.

My first movie is called *Beach Ball*, and the movie company decided to have opening day at a beach town. My mother, who likes me to call her Priscilla, is taking me to the opening day press conference.

"I hope you memorized all the answers I gave you to the reporters' questions," Priscilla said as the limo sped along the narrow ocean road. "I don't want you blurting out anything that comes into your head."

I wanted to say, "Please listen to me. I'm not Jonah. I'm not your son." But I had already said it at least ten times, and she didn't seem to ever hear a word I said.

So, I was Jonah Quicken now, at least for the time being. And I was about to walk a red carpet and get up on a stage in front of a hundred screaming girls.

Maybe you think I was happy about this. But you are wrong. I never wanted to be a star. The whole thing totally stressed me out. It felt like there were a dozen snakes slithering round and round in my belly, and my legs were shaking like Jell-O, even though I was sitting in a car.

This wasn't the life I wanted. I just wanted a life with nicer friends, and a brother who didn't bounce me off the wall every time he saw me, and parents who didn't blame me for everything that happened in the world.

"When you talk, remember to tilt your head so that your long hair falls over the short side," Pricilla instructed. "The girls go nuts every time you do that."

"I'll try to remember," I said. I rubbed a hand over the shaved side of my head.

The limo rolled past a Crab Shack drive-in. "Priscilla, I'm really hungry," I said. "Do we have time to stop for lunch?"

Her eyes went wide. "Lunch? Jonah, you know you're on a juice cleanse. You have to get rid of the extra two pounds you put on in Cancún."

Huh? Two extra pounds?

I was in Cancún?

"My stomach is growling," I said. "Can't I have anything?"

"I'm going to let you have some mixed berries for dinner tonight," she said, "*if* you do a good job at the press conference."

"Can I have them right after the movie?"

She shook her head. "No way. I made a gym appointment for you, Jonah. Look at your arms. You've totally neglected them. They are not going to want you for *Beach Ball II* with those arms."

She punched my chest. "I'm not even mentioning your six-pack. Once this tour is over, you have a lot of work in store with your trainer."

My trainer?

"We may have to change your schedule," Priscilla said. "Two hours a day in the gym may not be enough for you. Even if you do an extra workout at home every night after dinner."

Two hours of working out in the gym and a few mixed berries for dinner? This new life was only an hour old, but I was already starting to hate it.

"Here's something else we have to do," she continued. "Maybe after you do your Instagram and TikTok videos. Both of your managers think you should get small tattoos on the backs of your hands. Stars, maybe. Or snakes. You decide. It will get us a lot of press and TV coverage."

I gasped. "Mom—I'm fourteen!" I cried. "Do I have to get tattoos on my hands?"

"Please don't call me Mom," she snapped. "Try to remember, okay?" She fluffed up her blond hair with both hands.

"We're getting close," the driver said.

"Park a block away from the movie theater," she told him. "Jonah, you stay in the car. I'm going to walk up to the theater and make sure everything has been done right."

A few seconds later, the driver pulled the car over to the curb in front of a patch of tall pine trees. Priscilla waited for him to come around and open the door for her. She slid out, then turned back to me.

"Don't let anyone see you, Jonah," she said. "While I'm gone, you can practice the answers I gave you for the press conference."

The driver closed her door, and I watched her hurry

down the sidewalk toward the movie theater. The driver walked over to the pine trees and settled down in the shade.

I couldn't practice the answers she gave me because I never heard them. But I knew what I had to do.

The thought of standing up in front of reporters and a hundred screaming girls was giving me the deep shudders. I couldn't handle it. This whole new life wasn't for me.

I know, I know. A lot of kids would *kill* for the life of a superstar. I should be *thrilled* to go from my boring life where even my dog didn't like me to the fabulous, glam life of Jonah Quicken.

But it wasn't for me.

For one thing, I'm too shy. And for another thing . . . maybe I am too lazy. Two hours in the gym every day? A bowl of berries for dinner?

I shut my eyes and begged: *Please, please, when I open them, let me be ME again.*

But, of course, that didn't work.

I needed help. How could I get back to being Munroe Lackwitz?

My hands were ice-cold and dripping wet. I wiped them on the legs of my pants. My hand stopped when I realized I had a phone in my pocket.

Was it my phone? Or Jonah's?

It didn't matter. It meant I could call home. I could tell Mom or Dad to come rescue me.

I pulled the phone out with a trembling hand. The limo driver was leaning against a tree with his eyes closed. He couldn't see me.

It took two tries to punch in the number because my fingers were shaking so hard. The phone rang once . . . twice . . .

Come on! Come on! I begged. *I need help—fast!*

Mom answered after the third ring. "Hello?"

"Mom—it's me! I need help. I need you to come get me." The words burst out of me in a breathless rush.

"Who is this?" she asked.

"It's me. Munroe. You have to come and—"

"You want to speak to Munroe? He isn't home. He went camping with his dad."

"No!" I cried. "No way. *I am Munroe.* Don't you recognize me, Mom?"

"Who is this?" She sounded very confused. "Is this Devin? Didn't Munroe tell you he was going camping?"

"It's me, Mom. Please—believe me." My voice cracked on the words. "I need to be rescued. I'm in a new life, and I hate it. I need to come home."

"Devin, is this one of your jokes?" she asked. "Munroe told me about your jokes. Do you want to leave a message for Munroe?"

"No. No message. Please—"

I stopped. Out the front windshield, I saw Priscilla

striding back to the limo. A choking sound escaped my throat. I struggled to catch my breath.

"I'm outta here," I muttered. I clicked off the phone and jammed it into my pants pocket. Then I shoved open my car door and leaped out.

I lowered my head like a football runner and took off. My designer sneakers slapped the asphalt road as I sped away from the limo, heading back toward Sandy Harbor.

What did I plan to do? How far did I plan to run?

I had no plan. I had no thought in my head—except to escape from Priscilla and the driver.

I'm not much of a runner. After a minute or two, I was already panting for breath and holding my side. I glanced back—and saw the limo coming along the road toward me. With a cry, I dove behind some pine trees and ducked low.

The car sped past, black windows shining under the sun. They didn't see me.

I jogged back onto the road—and a miracle happened. A yellow taxi came rolling up. Amazed, I waved wildly, and it stopped. Did I have any money? I reached for my back pants pocket and felt a wallet. My hands trembled so hard, I could barely open it.

Yes! Yes! It was packed with twenty-dollar bills.

I leaped into the cab. And suddenly, I had a plan. My head cleared, my eyes focused. And I knew what I had to do.

I was never so excited to see the little stone building that housed the Sandy Harbor library. I slapped a bunch of twenties into the cab driver's hand, slammed the door, and practically flew up the front steps.

Hannah Green looked up from the front desk as I ran breathlessly into the room. "Hi. I . . . need a book," I choked out.

She squinted at me. "Well, you've come to the right place."

I leaned my hands on the desk in front of her, struggling to catch my breath. "No. I need a book called—"

"Hey—!" she interrupted me. "I think I know who you are! I'm a big fan."

I swept the long side of my hair over the shaved side. "Thank you," I said. "But I'm kind of in a hurry. The book is called *You Can Change Your Life*. I need it right away—"

Hannah studied me. "I know you probably get tired of people asking. But do you think I could have your autograph?"

"Sure, sure," I said, tapping my hands on the desk. "But the book—"

She finally stopped staring at me and tapped some keys

on the keyboard in front of her. "What did you say the book is called?"

"*You Can Change Your Life*," I repeated.

She typed some more and gazed into her monitor screen. "Uh . . . hmm . . ."

"What's the matter?" I asked.

"We only have one copy, and that book is checked out," she said.

I let out a groan. "Checked out?"

She nodded. "Yes. A boy named Munroe Lackwitz signed it out."

Oh, wow.

The book must be at my house. All I had to do was go home, read those weird words in it again—and I could change back into my old life.

"Jonah, do you think you could sign my arm?" Hannah asked, raising it to the desk top. "Or is that too weird? Can we take a selfie?"

"Maybe later," I replied. I spun away and darted out of the library.

The twenty-minute walk to my house seemed to take hours. The afternoon sun was setting. A strong wind blew off the ocean, and seagulls squawked at me from the beach, as if warning me away.

A red SUV rumbled past me, filled with teenagers, and they called, "Jonah! Jonah!" out the open windows.

Not for long, I thought. *Soon, I'll be changed back. And I'll be happier. I'll be grateful and not so down on my life.*

No cars in the driveway. My heart started to thud in my chest as I let myself in through the kitchen door. "Anyone home? Mom? Dad?" I shouted, racing to the front of the house.

No answer.

Frankie appeared in the den doorway and started to growl.

"It's me," I said. "Don't you recognize me?"

But, of course, he didn't. I was a stranger.

The dog didn't attack or anything. He's a terrible watchdog. He just sat there growling.

I pulled myself up the stairs two at a time and dove into my room. My eyes scanned from one wall to the other. "Where are you, book?" I said. "Where are you? I need you!"

I didn't see it anywhere. I crossed to my desk and began tossing books and papers to the floor, desperately searching. "Where are you? Where?"

I moved to my bookshelves against the back wall and glanced from title to title. My books were a mess, all just jammed in on their sides, upside down, and piled every which way. I didn't see it.

"Where *are* you?"

I let out a gasp when I saw it. Poking out from under

my pillow on the bed. "Yes!" I grabbed it and held it tightly in both hands. "Yes!"

I raised it to my face and read the title out loud. "*You Can Change Your Life.*" My voice was Jonah Quicken's voice. But not for long.

Breathing so hard my chest heaved up and down, I flipped frantically through the pages of the little book until I found the last page. The page with the strange words.

I took a deep breath. I swallowed. My mouth was as dry as cotton. I swallowed again. Squinted at the page. And read the words in a trembling voice:

"Glawson . . . Parkwallaby . . . Monostartic . . . Groostic . . . Maladonia . . . Freepnovia."

The room started to spin. I struggled to keep my balance.

The book fell from my hands and bounced across the rug. Then everything went white. And then a flickering red. Then black.

Did it work? DID it?

I opened my eyes. I was down on all fours. I sniffed the rug. It had a strong odor, like detergent or something. I gazed up at my bed. It seemed high above me.

I sniffed the air. And pawed at a long string of lint on the rug.

Huh? Why was I pawing on lint?

I made my way on all fours to the shiny white

wastebasket next to my desk. Then I raised my head and peered at my reflection on the side of the wastebasket.

I stared at my reflection—and then let out a howl of horror.

I was a dog. I was Frankie.

The book had changed my life again. The words had turned me into a dog.

No. No. No way.

I had to change this immediately. Where was the book? Where?

I sniffed the air. I could smell the book nearby. It had bounced under the bed.

I trotted across the room, ducked my head under the bed, and pawed at the book until it slid out.

No way I'm staying a dog. No way. I'm changing back to a human. I'm changing back to me.

I lowered my gaze to the book on the rug. I concentrated on the cover title in big black letters. Concentrated . . .

And started to whimper as I realized:

I'M A DOG. I CAN'T READ.

That's when Mom poked her head into the room. "Frankie!" she cried. "What are you doing up here in Munroe's room? Hey—leave his book alone!"

THE BAD SIDE

A friend and I were talking on the phone. He said, "I was surprised to see you at that party last week. I know you don't like to dance. But you were really rocking."

I felt a bit of a shock. "I wasn't at a party last week," I said.

"Yes, you were," my friend insisted. "I waved to you and you waved back."

My mind started to spin. *Do I have a double? Is there someone out there who looks just like me?*

I stared at myself in the mirror. *Is it possible that there are TWO of me?*

The face in the mirror stared back at me. "Good idea for a story," he said.

"CARSON, RAKING LEAVES IS A TOTAL WASTE OF TIME. WE'LL
rake them all up, and next week it will look like we
didn't rake," Mike said, tilting his rake up so he could
lean on it.

"I knew you were going to say that," I said. Mike and I
have been friends for a long time, and I pretty much know
what he's going to say. If I say something that isn't about
skateboarding or food, he's usually against it.

The funny thing is, Mike is almost always surprised by
whatever I say or do.

"I *knew* you were going to say that you knew I was
going to say that," Mike replied. But I knew he didn't
know I was going to say it.

I dug the rake in and swept up another bunch of the
crackling brown leaves. I dragged them toward the pile I
had already started at the curb.

"If you help me," I told him, "we can get to the skate park a lot faster."

"Why are you doing this?" he asked. "Why didn't you say you were too busy or had other plans or something?"

"You know my dad hurt his back," I answered. "So I asked him what I could do to help out, and he said rake the leaves in the front yard."

Mike shook his head. "Carson, don't you ever get tired of being such a good guy?"

The question was typical Mike, but it made me laugh.

"Why doesn't your dad get a leaf blower?" he asked. He still hadn't raked a single leaf. "We could borrow my dad's leaf blower. We'd be done already."

"Dad says they are bad for the environment," I replied. "It's the reason he won't get a power mower, either."

"Does he churn his own butter?" Mike said.

"I knew you were going to say that," I told him. We've been studying Colonial days in our sixth-grade class, and Mike was fascinated by people churning their own butter.

"They had to work so hard in those days," he told Ms. Fenimore, our teacher.

"They didn't have skateboards," she said. "So they had more time on their hands."

She can be pretty funny.

I leaned into the rake and dragged another heap of dead leaves toward the curb. "Come on, dude," I said. "Help me out. It can be fun, you know? We'll make a huge mountain of leaves and let Ozzie out, and watch him jump into it."

Ozzie is a wiener dog, and he really can't jump. But he loves burying himself in dead leaves. It's a big thrill for him, and he always puts on a good show.

Mike rolled his eyes. "That's too much excitement," he said. He can be sarcastic a lot of the time. He sighed. "I really want to get to the park. I haven't had any time to try out my new board."

Mike finally saved up enough money to buy a street board. He had a cruiser that his cousin Ernie gave him. But the wheels on a cruiser are too big to do tricks.

"I promised Dad . . ." I said. I stopped to mop sweat off my forehead with the sleeve of my jacket.

"How about tomorrow? Sunday?" Mike said. "Can we get an early start before all the older guys get to the park?"

I shook my head. "I don't think so. I promised my parents I'd help them clean up the spare room. My grandparents are coming to stay for a week."

Mike sighed again. "Why don't you join the Boy Scouts, Carson? You could do good deeds all day long."

I started to answer, but I saw someone coming down the block. I recognized her red hair when she was still five houses down. Shannon Darby, a girl from our class.

She came speeding along the sidewalk on a silver scooter, her hair flying behind her. When she reached

Mike and me, she hopped off and let the scooter fall into the leaves.

"Hey—!" She swept her hair down with both hands. Her blue hoodie hung open. She wore a red-and-white school sweatshirt over black leggings.

"Don't you wear a helmet?" I asked.

She ignored my question. "You two raked all these?"

"One of us did," I said.

"Impressive." Shannon has green eyes, and they kind of twinkled in the afternoon sun.

"Carson, I still can't get over Lia Garcia's birthday party," she said.

I squinted at her. "Her birthday party?"

Her grin grew wider. "I mean, what you did at Lia's party."

"But—" I started. I only got that one word out.

Shannon erupted in words. "Sneaking into the other room and opening Lia's presents before she could? How could you do that, Carson? When we opened the door and saw you there on the floor with the ripped-up wrapping paper all around you and that guilty look on your face? It was *horrifying*. Ribbon tossed everywhere and all the gifts opened, and you holding one of Lia's new sweaters?"

"But—" I tried again.

"Why did you *do* that?" Shannon cried. "What were

you thinking, Carson? What on earth made you sneak in and do that? It's so totally unlike you!"

"But—but—"

Shannon stared hard at me. Before I could get a word out, she was back on her scooter and rolling away.

"Shannon—wait!" I called.

But she didn't even turn around. I watched her red hair bobbing behind her as she picked up speed and disappeared around the corner.

I turned back to Mike. He was studying me like he'd never seen me before.

I waited for my heartbeat to slow and my brain to stop spinning. Then I said, "There's only one problem with that story."

"Problem?" Mike repeated.

"Yes," I said. "I wasn't *at* Lia Garcia's birthday party."

The sun was already dropping behind the trees when Mike and I finally made it to the skateboard park. My arms were aching from all the leaf-work, and I had a splinter in my right thumb from the rake handle.

But I couldn't wait to get on my board and practice my ollies and nose ollies. Yes, I know those are the beginning basics. But Mike and I were still working on them. They're not as easy as they look, especially when you're just starting out.

Mike's new board was totally awesome. The deck had red and blue lightning bolts in all directions and the words *Street Shredder* in jagged letters. My smiley face deck suddenly looked seriously babyish to me, and I began to think of getting my parents to replace it.

The air was cool, and dark clouds rolled low overhead. Squinting into the dim light, the park appeared empty at first. But then I saw a kid down on his knees on the concrete.

His head bobbed up and down and he made weird wheezing sounds.

"What's up with him?" Mike said.

Gripping our boards at our sides, we both ran across the grass to where the kid was at the edge of the park.

I didn't recognize him. His face was bright red and his eyes bulged. When he saw us coming, he began to wave wildly with both hands.

"He's choking!" Mike cried. He grabbed at his pants pockets. "I—I don't have my phone. We can't call for help!"

"No problem," I said, trying to keep my voice calm. "I took a CPR class at camp last summer."

The boy's face had darkened to purple. He made horrible bleating sounds, like a goat stuck in a fence.

I spun behind him and wrapped my arms around his

waist. Then I gripped my hands together and *punched* his belly as hard as I could.

I heard a *pop* sound—and a big purple wad came flying from his open mouth.

Bubble gum!

I eased my arms around his belly, then lowered them to my sides. The boy wheezed loudly for a while. He took a deep breath and then another. A few seconds later, he smiled as he began to breathe normally.

Mike slapped my shoulder. "Wow, Carson, you saved his life!"

"That's what CPR is all about," I said. My heart was pounding. I climbed to my feet.

"Th-thank you," the boy stammered. He picked up his skateboard. "That was a close one. I . . . couldn't breathe at all."

"Glad you're okay," I said. "You here by yourself?"

He shook his head. His face was still red. "My friend was here, but he left. Guess I should have gone with him."

He thanked me a few more times. Then he ran off, carrying his board under his arm.

"One more good deed for you," Mike said. "Hey, why do you look so weird?"

"I'm a little shaken up," I said. "I mean . . . what if that hadn't worked? What would we—"

I stopped because I saw two guys hurrying toward

us on their boards. Rory and Scott. Two guys from the high school. They were here at the skateboard park all the time, always telling Mike and me to stay out of their space.

They both had scowls on their faces as they rolled up to us. Rory narrowed his eyes at me. "Hey, did you forget already?" he said. "Or are you just being a wise guy?"

I backed up a step. "Wise guy? Me?"

He gave my chest a shove with both hands. "I told you this morning not to come back here," he said. "I warned you, didn't I? "You're not welcome here anymore."

I made a startled cry. "Huh? This morning?"

"Don't even," Scott said, stepping up beside Rory. He had his fists at his sides, as if he was ready to fight.

"I—I don't understand," I stammered. "Why—?"

"We caught you, dude," Rory said. "Stealing that little kid's board."

"Did you really think no one was watching?" Scott demanded.

"Your board is babyish," Rory said. "But that's no excuse to try to take a little kid's board."

"That kid was crying his eyes out," Scott said.

Rory shoved me again. "Take a hike. I mean seriously. Don't come back. Don't let us see you here again."

"But—but—" I sputtered. "I wasn't *here* this morning!"

"He's telling the truth," Mike said. "I was with him all morning. We were raking leaves in his front yard. We just got here."

"Don't lie for your friend," Rory said, turning on Mike. "Scott and I both saw your pal here. We caught him in the act."

"Th-that's impossible," I stammered. "It must have been someone who looked like me. I was home raking leaves. You can ask my parents."

"I don't have to ask anyone," Rory said. "It was you. Now, get lost. And don't come back."

"Don't make us get violent," Scott said, curling and uncurling his fists. "Rory and I don't like violence. And we don't like thieves."

"You're making a big mistake," Mike said.

"You're making a mistake by staying here," Scott shot back.

I grabbed Mike's sleeve. "Let's go," I muttered, shaking my head. I tucked my board under my arm and started to walk away.

Mike followed right behind. "Those two guys are bad news," he said. "What's up with them?"

"Beats me," I replied. "Beats me."

"Something totally strange is going on," I said. "People keep seeing me in places where I'm not there."

It was the next day, and Mike and I were in my room. We had started to play *Minecraft*, one of our new obsessions. But I just couldn't keep my mind on it.

Mike sat on the edge of my desk, the game controller in front of him in one hand. I sprawled on the floor, leaning my back against the bed.

Mike turned away from the screen and gazed around the room. "Where are your clothes?" he asked. "Don't you toss them on the floor like I do?"

"No way," I said. "I hang everything up in my closet or put stuff in the dresser."

Mike blew out a whoosh of air. "Carson, you are too good to be true," he said.

I shrugged. "I just like a neat room. What's the big deal?" I sighed. "I can't stop thinking about yesterday. It's such a total mystery."

Mike nodded. "Yeah. A mystery."

"I would never try to steal a kid's board," I said. "You know that isn't like me at all."

"We weren't there," Mike said. "It has to be a mistake."

"It's so weird," I said. "First, Shannon said she saw me at Lia Garcia's birthday party, and I opened Lia's presents before she could. And I wasn't at that party. I wasn't even invited."

"Weird," Mike said.

"Then this whole thing with the kid's skateboard," I continued. "You and I both know I wasn't at the skate park."

Mike stared at me but didn't reply. What could he say?

"How can I be two places at once?" I demanded. "It's impossible, right?"

Mike slid down off the desktop. "We need to do something to take our minds off this," he said. "Let's go to Meckler's and get ice cream cones or something."

Meckler's is a little candy store and lunch counter a block from our school where everyone hangs out. Mr. Meckler is a friend of my parents. Whenever he is there, I always get an extra ice cream scoop on my cone.

Mike and I tugged on our jackets and made our way outside. "See? I told you raking leaves is a waste of time," Mike said.

He was right. The front lawn was covered in dead brown leaves again. A strong wind was sending more leaves tumbling down from the trees.

Our shoes crunched over the leaves as we walked to the store. It was still a few weeks before Halloween. But some people were out decorating their houses. We waved to Shannon's parents as we passed their yard. They were propping up a scarecrow on a tall pole.

I was shivering when we arrived at Meckler's. "Maybe

a hot chocolate instead of ice cream," I said, pulling open the front door.

The air was warm inside the little store and smelled of hamburgers and fries. Two women sat having coffee on stools at the far end of the lunch counter.

Mr. Meckler came hurrying from behind the counter to greet us. He is a big man with a round face and a beach ball stomach that bounces beneath his chef's apron.

His smile faded as he stepped up to Mike and me. "I'm sorry, Carson," he said. "But I told you I don't want you in my store anymore."

I gasped. "Uh . . . *whaaat?*"

"I told you this morning," he said. "I promised I wouldn't tell your parents. But I can't have you coming in here to steal things."

"Wait! What?" I cried. "I don't understand. I—"

"Do I really have to remind you?" he said. "The four candy bars I found in your coat pocket that you weren't going to pay for?"

"No! No way!" I said. "Mr. Meckler, I wasn't here this morning. You know I don't steal. I—I—"

"You didn't even make up an excuse," he said. "I caught you red-handed. And you didn't say anything. You really thought I'd let you get away with it."

Mike squinted at me. I could see he was as confused and bewildered as I was.

I could feel my face grow burning hot, and I knew I was blushing. "It wasn't me," I said. "Seriously—"

Mr. Meckler held the door open. "Bye, Carson. Sorry. Hope you've learned a lesson."

I said goodbye to Mike and walked home by myself. I didn't want to talk about what just happened. I wanted to sit in my room and think, and try to make sense of what was going on.

"Where were you?" Mom called from the living room when I stepped into the house.

"Just went for a walk," I called. I hurried to my room.

And stopped in shock at the open doorway.

"Huh?" I stared at the pile of wrinkled-up clothes on the floor and books and papers scattered over my bed. And what was that on my pillow? A half-eaten slice of pizza?

I stepped into the room and saw the boy sitting at my desk. He had a spilled soda can in front of him, and his chin was smeared in pizza sauce.

He was me. I mean, he looked exactly like me, except his hair was messed up, and he had a big stain on the front of his T-shirt.

"Hey—!" he called out when he saw me enter the room. He burped. "Where you been?"

"Wh-who *are* you?" I cried. "What are you doing in my room?"

My questions made him laugh. He burped again and chewed off another hunk of pizza from the slice in his hand.

"Who *are* you?" I repeated. I couldn't take my eyes off him. He really was my exact double.

"Don't you know?" he replied. He grinned at me. "Can't you figure it out?"

I stood there with my mouth hanging open.

He set the pizza slice down on my laptop keyboard. "I thought you were smarter than that, Poop Face."

"Don't call me Poop Face," I said.

"Guess I have to tell you who I am," he said, "since you can't figure it out."

I shoved my hands into my pockets. "Tell me," I said.

His eyes locked on mine. "I'm your bad side," he said.

"My *what*?" I cried.

"Your bad side," he said. "You kept me bottled up for so long, I finally had to come out."

"I—I don't understand," I stammered.

He sighed. "You're always so good, Carson. Always such a perfect kid. You kept me—your bad side—bottled up inside you. I was like a prisoner. Watching you be such a goody-goody."

I stared hard at him, my thoughts spinning.

"Finally, I had to break out," he said. "I couldn't take it anymore. We all have two sides, Carson. A good side and a bad side. But you wouldn't let me be me. I had no choice. I had to break free."

"No!" I cried, my voice cracking. "I don't want you here. You are wrecking my life. You have to go."

He shrugged. "Go? Where would I go? I'm part of you."

"No way!" I screamed. "Get out! Get out of my room! Disappear! You have to disappear—now!"

He laughed. "I'm out now. And I'm going to stay out. Deal with it."

I could feel myself losing it. "Go!" I screamed. "Go! I mean it!"

"You can't make me," he said, lowering his voice to a growl. "How are you going to make me, Carson?"

And in that instant, I knew how to get rid of him.

It came to me in a flash. A flash of anger—and fear.

I knew it was the only way to make him disappear.

I rushed across the room and grabbed my pillow. I lifted the pizza slice and smeared the tomato sauce into the pillowcase. Then I pulled off the pillowcase and began to rip the pillow apart, sending feathers flying over the floor. I tore the sheets off my bed and heaved them to the floor.

"Hey—what do you think you're doing?" my bad side cried.

I ignored him and darted to my closet. I began tugging

out shirts and pants, and I tossed them in a heap on the floor. I knocked over my dresser and watched my stuff come falling out of the drawers.

"Stop!" my bad side shouted. His voice came out thin and shaky. He was starting to sound weaker. "Stop it!"

I grabbed the pizza slice he had been eating and smeared it over my laptop screen. Then I knocked the lamp off my desk and sent it crashing to the floor in an explosion of glass.

"Stop . . . please," my bad side whispered. And then he disappeared. Vanished with a soft pop of air.

Gone.

I stood struggling to catch my breath, looking at all the damage I had done. Sweat poured down my forehead. My whole body felt shaky.

But I had won. I knew the only way to get rid of him was to be badder than he was. If I was bad, he had no reason to exist. He had no choice but to disappear.

"Oh no!"

I heard a shriek from my bedroom doorway. I spun around to see Mom, eyes bulging in horror, mouth hanging open as she gazed at the mess in my room.

"Carson—what *happened* here?" she cried.

"I . . . I can explain," I said.

She pressed her hands at her waist and stood waiting. "Well . . . go ahead."

"Uh . . . actually, I *can't* explain," I said.

She stared at me. "You just went berserk and destroyed your room for no reason?"

"Well . . . I had a *good* reason," I said. "Please trust me, Mom. It will never happen again."

Or will it??

THE HOLE
IN THE GROUND

This story started in my backyard when I tripped on the grass. I looked down and saw that a small hole in the ground had made me stumble.

I bent down to examine the hole. Was it a rabbit hole?

I'm a big Bugs Bunny cartoon fan, and I pictured a rabbit down the hole hiding a big supply of carrots.

Of course, the hole might have been made by a mole, or a field mouse, or some other animal. It was a mystery.

And it became more mysterious the next day when I discovered the hole had grown larger—wider and deeper. I stared at it. Could it be some kind of sinkhole? Or were several creatures living down there beneath my lawn?

I felt a chill at the back of my neck. And I challenged myself: Can I write a scary story about a simple hole in the ground?

And that's how this story came to be.

KENDRA AND MAX SHOWED ME THE HOLE BEHIND MY GARAGE ON my first weekend at our new house.

Since I was new in the neighborhood, I didn't know them well. But they talked to me in school, and I thought we could probably become good friends.

Kendra lives across the street from me in a little house perched behind a tall hedge at the sidewalk. Max's house is on the next block. I haven't seen it yet.

Another boy, named Oliver, tried to be friendly on the first day of school. But he had an odd giggle and a hoarse, froggy voice, and he kept shoving his hands into his pockets, then pulling them out. Like he was nervous.

He followed me around for a few days. I could see that he was lonely. But he kind of creeped me out, and I didn't want to be his friend.

My name is Adam Persky. Kendra, Max, and I are in

fifth grade at Bell City Middle School. Kendra is tall and thin, at least six inches taller than me. She has curly red hair and freckles on her cheeks.

Max has long black hair and wears glasses. He doesn't smile much. He always appears to be thinking hard about something. He is taller than me, too.

Mom says I'll probably have a growth spurt in sixth or seventh grade. She says maybe then I'll lose my baby fat, too. Mom has a cold sense of humor.

On Saturday afternoon, Max and Kendra showed up at my house. I was glad to see them. I'd been helping my parents unpack cartons all day, and I needed an excuse to get away.

Don't let anyone tell you that moving to a new house is exciting or fun. It's a lot of hard work, hauling stuff out of cartons, then finding a place to put it all. I couldn't find the posters for my room. And I didn't even know what box my PlayStation was in.

A new house can also be a little scary. I'm not the kind of guy who jumps at every sound or gets the shakes watching scary movies. But our new house makes creaks and bumps and groans and cracks at night. I hear every one. I haven't been able to sleep since we moved in.

Anyway, I'm sure I'll get used to the noises. I'm not a scaredy-cat. I just have good ears. And maybe my imagination is also too good.

I pulled Max and Kendra into the living room and introduced them to Mom and Dad. My parents were both bent over moving cartons. They said hi without looking up.

"Oh, look," Mom said, lifting something from her carton. "Adam, this is the old teddy bear you used to hold when you sucked your thumb."

I rolled my eyes. I could feel my cheeks growing hot. "Nice, Mom. I'm sure Kendra and Max love seeing my old teddy bear."

Kendra and Max both laughed.

Mom didn't stop. "One day I found you sitting totally naked on the couch, hugging your teddy bear and—"

"That's *enough!*" I shouted.

I knew what she was doing. She was deliberately embarrassing me, just for fun. I told you Mom has a cold sense of humor.

"Why don't you go outside and get some fresh air?" Dad said, wiping sweat off his forehead with one sleeve.

So that's what we did.

"I want to show you something," Kendra said. She led the way up the gravel driveway to the back of the garage. The back of our SUV was open, and I could see stacks of glass flower vases packed inside.

"Wow. Your parents must really like flowers," Max said.

"Dad is a flower freak," I told him. "Actually, he has an

excuse. He's a scientist. A botanist. He studies plants at a lab at the university."

"Flowers make me sneeze," Kendra said. She tilted her head back and let out a loud sneeze. "See?" she said. "Even *thinking* about flowers makes me sneeze!"

She pulled me around the corner of the garage. The grass was patchy back here, and there were a lot of tall weeds. A wooden fence ran along the back of our yard. Some of the boards had been knocked down, and there were a lot of pieces missing.

"What are we doing back here?" I asked.

Kendra pointed to a patch of dirt. "Look at this, Adam."

She and Max both squatted down and lowered their eyes to the circle of dirt in the grass.

I squatted down beside Max. "What are you looking at? That hole in the ground?"

They both nodded.

I squinted at it. The hole was three or four inches deep and about as wide as a bucket or a paint can. "Awesome," I said sarcastically. "Is this what you do for fun around here? You stare at holes in the dirt?"

Kendra raised her eyes to mine. "Not for fun," she replied in a whisper.

I blinked. Something about her stare gave me a chill.

Max climbed to his feet. He glanced down the driveway, as if checking to see if anyone could hear us. "I hope it isn't like the hole Kendra and I found a few weeks ago," he said.

"What *about* the hole you found?" I demanded.

Kendra stood up and brushed off the legs of her jeans. "Let's not talk about it," she said, still in a whisper. "Let's just keep an eye on this hole."

I stared at them both. At their grim faces. Their wide, frightened eyes.

"Okay. I get it," I said. "This is *trick the new guy*. Do you play this joke on everyone who moves here? You get them to stare at holes in the ground?"

They didn't crack a smile. "It isn't a joke," Kendra said.

"Okay. Show me the hole you both found a few weeks ago," I said.

They both gasped.

"No. We can't go back there," Max said.

"We can never go back there," Kendra whispered.

I knew they were joking, seeing if they could scare me. "Let's go somewhere," I said. I started walking toward the street.

We ended up at the playground behind the school. Max and Kendra met up with some kids they knew. I joined them and we started throwing a couple of Frisbees around.

I saw the kid named Oliver leaning against a tree near the sidewalk. He was all by himself, watching us. I could tell he wanted to join the group. But I didn't say anything.

After the Frisbee game broke up, I followed Max and Kendra to a little store a few blocks away, and we bought candy bars. "I'm a chocolate freak," she said.

"You're just a freak!" Max said.

"And what are *you*?" she shot back.

I could tell they've been friends for a long time.

"I want to explore the neighborhood more," I said, rubbing a smear of chocolate off my chin. "I don't know where anything is."

Max glanced up at the sky. The sun was dropping behind the trees. "Can't," he said. "I have to be home by dark."

"Me too," Kendra said.

They walked me home, then hurried away without saying goodbye or anything. I watched them running across the front yards. "Hey! See you in school!" I shouted after them.

The kitchen wasn't unpacked yet, so we went to a fried chicken place in town. My parents are both *terrible* cooks, so I love it when we go out somewhere to eat.

I sat across from them in the booth and grabbed two breasts and a leg. I could have eaten the entire bucket!

Dad sighed. "I unpacked so many boxes, I can barely raise my arms."

Mom turned to me. "Tomorrow we'll finish your room," she said.

I swallowed some mashed potatoes. "Did you find my PlayStation?" I asked.

"Not yet," Mom said. "But I think I know what box it's in." She frowned at me. "Don't look like that, Adam. It's there. We didn't leave your precious PlayStation behind."

Dad ripped apart a wing. "Adam, what were you three kids doing behind the garage?" he asked.

"Nothing," I said. "I mean . . . they wanted to show me a hole in the ground."

Dad swallowed. "Excuse me? A hole?"

"What was special about it?" Mom asked.

"Nothing," I said. "I think it was a joke. They were trying to frighten me."

"Frighten you about a hole in the ground? That's ridiculous," Dad said.

Was it ridiculous?

I would soon find out.

A couple of days went by before I saw the hole again.

Why did I go back to look at it? I was in the lunchroom with Kendra and Max that afternoon, and Max asked me if I'd looked behind my garage lately.

He and Kendra shared a giggle. Like they had a private joke.

"You're both not funny," I said. "You're not going to scare me with that 'hole in the ground' joke."

But sure enough, after school, I walked up the driveway, my shoes crunching on the gravel, and made my way to the back of the garage.

The hole was definitely bigger. It was maybe three to four feet wide. Wide enough for me to step into the center of it. And it was deeper. At least two feet deep. Halfway up to my knees.

I stood in the middle of the hole and chuckled. Max and Kendra were definitely going to a lot of trouble to scare me with their hole prank.

I glanced around the backyard, searching for the shovel they had used to dig the hole deeper and wider. I didn't see one. They must have taken it with them.

"No way I'm going to fall for this," I muttered to myself. I climbed out of the hole and started to the kitchen door.

Before I reached it, Dad's car rolled up the drive. He climbed out and waved to me. "Hey, Adam—what are you doing back here?"

"Dad, I want to show you something," I said. I motioned for him to follow me.

He set down his briefcase and raincoat and came striding after me to the back of the garage. "What's up?"

"Look." I pointed to the hole in the ground.

He gazed at it for a few seconds, then turned to me.

"It's a hole," he said. "Looks like the previous owner wanted to build something back here. Or maybe plant a tree."

I shook my head. "You don't understand," I said. "It's much bigger than before. I was back here with Max and Kendra, remember? And it was a tiny hole? And now—"

"Oh. Right. I remember." Dad grinned. "You said they were trying to scare you. I guess they sneaked back here and dug the hole deeper. Your friends are real jokers."

He started back toward the house. I chased after him. "I'm not so sure it was Max and Kendra," I said. "Do you think it could be a sinkhole?"

Dad stopped. "A sinkhole?"

"I saw a video about sinkholes," I said. "The ground just opens up and swallows whole cars and stuff."

"We don't get sinkholes up here," Dad says. "That's mostly in Florida, where the ground is a lot softer."

So it had to be a bad joke.

When I saw Max and Kendra in school the next morning, I didn't even mention it. I didn't want them to know that I'd seen the hole. And I definitely didn't want them to know that I couldn't get to sleep that night because I was thinking about the hole and picturing it growing bigger and bigger.

After school, we met those same kids from the playground and started another Frisbee-tossing session. I can put a pretty good spin on the Frisbee. But Kendra is the best, mainly because she's so tall.

Max sent one flying, and it sailed over my head toward the street. I leaped up, made a grab for it, and missed. I spun around and chased after it. And once again, I glimpsed that kid Oliver, leaning against a tree and watching us.

I felt bad. I could see he was lonely. He was always by himself. *Maybe we should invite him to join us*, I thought. *He can probably use some friends.*

I started to mention it to the others. But I stopped when I saw Oliver step away from the tree. He came walking toward us, his hands jammed in his jeans pockets. His dark hair fell over his eyes, but I could see he was staring at me.

"I think he wants to join us," I said to Kendra.

"Hey, you—!"

I was surprised by Oliver's angry shout.

"What are *you* looking at?" he yelled.

He stepped up to me, so close I had to back up. "What are you looking at, dude?" he shouted into my face. "You've been staring at me ever since you came here."

"N-no," I stammered. "I haven't. I just—"

"What's your problem?" he snapped. "Why have you been watching me? Something you want to say to me?" He pulled his fists from his jeans pockets.

Max stepped in front of me. "No one is staring at you, Oliver," he said. "Back off. Do you always imagine people are looking at you?"

Oliver's chest was heaving up and down. He was breathing noisily. He grabbed my arm. "Come over here."

He dragged me over to the trees. Then he stared hard at me, his dark eyes locking on mine. "You're the new kid, right?"

"Right," I said.

He looked over my shoulder at Max and Kendra. "Did they tell you about the secrets of Bell City?" he demanded.

"S-secrets?" I stammered. "No. I—"

"This town isn't what it seems," Oliver said, narrowing his eyes. "If they tell you about some strange things . . . believe them."

I took a step back. "I . . . don't know what you mean," I said.

He grabbed my arm again. "Adam, do you have a hole in your backyard?"

"Uh . . . yes," I said. "How do you know about that?"

His eyes burned into mine. "I'm just saying," he murmured. "There are secrets you should know about."

Then he let go of my arm, lowered his gaze, turned, and stomped away.

I hurried back to Max and Kendra. My heart was pounding. "Weird," I muttered.

"Seriously weird," Max said. "I don't know what his problem is. He's always starting things."

"I'll watch out for him," I said.

On Saturday, Kendra said she and Max wanted to show me a special place. We put on swimsuits and rode our bikes past the town. A dirt road led us along a sandy path to a large round lake, sparkling in the afternoon sun.

We parked our bikes against a tree and walked onto the shore. I saw families having picnics on blankets and a few kids splashing in the water.

"This is Looking Glass Lake," Kendra explained. "Look at the water. It's as clear as a looking glass. Awesome?"

"Awesome," I agreed.

"Let's swim," Max said.

I held back. "My parents don't like me to swim unless there's an adult watching."

Max pointed. "There's a lifeguard. See?"

I turned and saw a young woman in a red swimsuit sitting on a high lifeguard chair. She had a whistle hanging from her neck, and her eyes were on the kids in the water. "Okay. Let's go," I said.

The three of us took off, running over the sand to the

water. I shivered as it rose to my waist. The water was clear and cold.

I kicked off from the soft, grassy bottom and dove underwater, pulling myself out deeper. Kendra and Max floated at my sides. "This is awesome!" I cried as I bobbed to the surface.

"It's great to have a lake so close," Kendra said. "Where did you used to swim, Adam?"

"I learned to swim at the Y," I answered. "We didn't have any lake or river or anything nearby." I lifted my legs and floated on my back. "I'm beginning to like this town."

The water had matted Kendra's red hair against her face. She glanced at Max, then turned to me. "Have you looked at the hole in your backyard?"

"Yeah," Max said. "When is the last time you checked it?"

I groaned. "Isn't that joke getting a little old?"

They looked at each other. "Joke?" they both said.

I ducked underwater. I didn't want to think about a hole in the ground. I wanted to enjoy my swim.

The water was so clear. I opened my eyes. I could see Max and Kendra from below the surface. I love to swim. Having a lake this close to home made me very excited.

I didn't want to get out. I wanted to stay here forever. But I knew my parents expected me home.

As we stepped back onto the shore, Kendra brushed

back her wet hair. She had a strange grin on her face. "Adam, tell the truth. Are you ever going to check the hole behind your garage?"

"No," I said. "I'm never going back there again."

That was a lie.

After dinner, Mom and Dad wanted to hang posters in my room. But I said I had to do something first. I closed the kitchen door behind me and walked quickly to the back of the garage.

"Whoa!" I exclaimed to myself when I saw how much the hole had grown.

It was wide now, as wide as a baseball pitcher's mound. I stepped up to the edge and peered down. How deep was it? I couldn't see the bottom. I saw only solid black all the way down.

I had to show this to Mom or Dad. I turned to go back to the house. But something stopped me.

Something held me there. Something made me turn back to the hole.

My breath caught in my throat as I peered straight down. How deep was it?

I stood on the edge. My legs suddenly trembled. I knew I was going to jump. Such a strong feeling. Such a powerful force, urging me forward. Urging me to jump into the hole.

I clamped my teeth together and struggled to pull back. I tried to resist. But the urge was too powerful.

With a gasp, I bent my knees and jumped into the hole.

I opened my mouth to scream as I plunged down. But no sound came out of my mouth. Down, down. How far was I falling?

I landed hard but stayed on my feet. Pain shot up from my ankles and roared up my entire body. I started to pant like a dog. I raised my eyes to the top of the hole. All I could see was a tiny circle of purple night sky high above me.

I can't tell you what happened next.

I know what happened. But it wouldn't be right to share it with you.

It was too horrifying.

I can tell you that I stood there trembling on the dirt floor. I wrapped my arms around my chest and hugged myself. I stared at the black dirt walls that circled me, thinking, *Why did I jump? Why did I do it?*

And then the hands poked out from the dirt wall. Bony hands all around me.

Fingers uncurled and pointed at me. The fingers stretched, grew longer. And sharp talons sprung from the long fingertips.

I spun around. They circled me. I had nowhere to turn. Nowhere to duck away from them.

The sharp talons began to poke me. Sharp needles. Poking me through my shirt. Tapping hard, then pushing into my skin. Long sharp needles poking my skin. Poking . . . Poking deeper.

Scream after scream burst from my throat. I don't know if my screams reached the top of the hole. I screamed so hard my throat throbbed with pain.

And then the poking stopped. The long needles slid back into the hands. And the hands pulled back into the dirt wall.

I shut my eyes tight, breathing hard, waiting for the pain to fade.

When I opened my eyes, I was back up on the ground. I stood on the edge of the hole, blinking and struggling to catch my breath.

I staggered back to safety. I pressed my back against the garage wall.

I felt different. The pain was gone. But I didn't feel like myself.

I raised my arms, and they stretched toward the back fence. They stretched longer and longer. I cried out when I saw dark fur on the backs of my hands.

I put my hands under my chin, pushed—and my head stretched two feet on my neck. A grumbling roar escaped my mouth. I waved my long rubbery arms and stared in disbelief at the fur that covered my hands.

What am I? Some kind of monster?

I had to show Max and Kendra. Why did they lead me to the hole? Why did they want this to happen to me?

Were they monsters, too?

I had planned to meet them at the playground. Running on all fours, I headed to the street, keeping close to the side of the house. I didn't want my parents to see me.

I tried to stay in the shadows as I scrambled toward the school. The wind brushed my fur as I ran. My hands and feet pounded the ground.

As I neared the playground, my brain was a frantic jumble of thoughts. *How could this happen? What will happen to me now? Why did Max and Kendra do this to me?*

Suddenly, I was back on two feet. The fur on my hands vanished into my skin. My arms and legs felt normal now. I could not stretch them.

Normal? Would I ever be normal?

I spotted Max and Kendra under a tree at the curb. They waved as I raced toward them. My heart beat so hard, my chest felt like it was bursting. I gasped for breath. My whole body trembled as I crossed the street and stepped up to them.

"The hole . . ." I struggled to speak. "The hole—"

Max laughed. "You look so frightened," he said. "You saw the hole?"

"I—I—I—"

Kendra laughed, too. "Oh, wow, Adam. Don't tell me you fell for our joke."

I swallowed. "Joke?"

They both nodded. "We were just trying to give you a scare," Kendra said. "Max and I kept digging it a little bigger every night. Did we fool you?"

"Did we *really* frighten you?" Max asked.

"But—but—" I struggled to find the words. "Oliver warned me—"

Max snickered. "Oliver is our best friend. He helped us dig the hole. And he said he did his best to scare you."

Kendra put a hand on my arm. "It's just a big hole in the ground, that's all," she said. "Did we really scare you?"

THE MONSTER-MAKER

When I was a kid, a lot of my friends enjoyed building models. They bought model airplane kits and model automobile kits, and spent hours and hours cutting and carving them, gluing them, carefully fitting the pieces together. Then painting and polishing their car or plane, ready to show it off with the rest of their model collection.

I wasn't interested. I could never figure out the instructions. I was clumsy with scissors, hopeless with the sharp little knives they all used, and couldn't paste or glue anything without getting my fingers stuck together.

I became interested in model building only after I saw the original, terrifying movie of *Frankenstein*. And I began to wonder: What would it be like to build a monster?

This story was inspired by that question.

"OW!" I CRIED OUT AND DROPPED THE MONSTER ONTO THE worktable. It clonked hard but didn't break.

My friend Annie Bender hurried across the garage to me. "What's wrong, Jamie?" she asked.

I sucked the spot of blood on my finger. "Cut myself. I didn't realize the talons are so sharp," I said.

She gazed at the long, curled talons poking out from the monster's big front paws. "Maybe you should file them down," she said.

"No. They might break," I replied. My finger stopped bleeding. "This monster has given me nothing but trouble," I said. I picked it up around the middle and raised it to Annie. "But it's worth it. This lizard monster is one of my best, don't you think?"

She studied it. "Maybe when you finish it," she said.

"I like your swamp monster best so far. The one with the yellow and green scales all over its body."

"You just like that one because you painted the scales," I said. Annie was supposed to be a helper, but sometimes she took over and finished the model monster without even asking me.

I didn't mind. We were a good team. Except when we fought about things, like what color to use, or how long the fangs should be, or what kind of fur to glue on.

I turned to the back wall of our garage and gazed at the shelves my dad built to hold my model monster collection. I started building monsters in fourth grade, three years ago. And now I have about two dozen monster creations in the collection.

I built some of the early monsters from kits. But all of the newer ones Annie and I made from scratch. Annie is a good artist, and she helps me sketch them out first. Then we figure out what we need to build them.

It's kind of a perfect hobby for me. Dad works in a lumber store, and Mom has her own fabric and sewing shop. So I have everything I need for monster building. Also, they never use the long worktable in the garage. So it is all mine.

My new lizard monster was pretty big, nearly two feet long. The mouth was open with two rows of long, white fangs. I ran my finger up and down its smooth back.

Through the open garage door, I could see the late

afternoon sun lowering itself behind the trees. A shadow stretched across the garage floor.

"Do you have to go home right away?" I asked Annie. "I need you to help me glue the fur on this one."

She blinked. "Excuse me? Fur? Why do you want to put fur on a lizard monster?"

"Because it would be different," I said. "I think a lizard covered in black fur would be scary."

"Definitely ugly," she said. She picked up the square of shaggy black carpet I planned to use for fur. "Is this what you want to glue on? Over its whole body?"

I nodded. "I cut it to fit," I said. "I just need you to wrap it around the lizard belly and hold it in place while I glue it."

"Fur on a lizard," she muttered. "You're weird, Jamie." She picked up the black rug. "It would be easier if you turn the rug over and spread the glue all over the back. Then put it on the model."

"That's a plan," I said.

I picked up the bottle of glue. It was one of those bottles with the brush stuck through the lid. I held the bottle in my right hand and tried to turn the lid with my left.

"Hey, it's stuck," I said. "Can't budge it."

"Try slamming the lid down on the worktable. Then turn it," Annie said.

"No. Wait. I think I got it." I squeezed the lid with all

my strength. It came toppling off, and the bottle slipped and tilted over my hand.

"Oh no!" I cried out as a wave of thick glue gushed onto my hand and poured onto the front of my T-shirt. "Oh, wow. I don't believe it!"

Annie burst out laughing. She has a sick sense of humor.

"It isn't funny!" I cried. "It's fast-drying glue. My fingers are sticking together. I can't get the bottle off my hand! Help me!"

She backed up. "No way! I'm not getting that glop on me! I'm not getting sticky!"

"But I'm stuck to the bottle!" I cried.

She gave my back a shove. "Quick. Get in the house and run warm water over it before it totally hardens."

So that's what I did. I ran to the bathroom sink and ran hot water over my hand until the glue loosened. Annie didn't help at all. She just handed me a towel when the glue was finally gone.

We walked back to the garage to clean up the rest of the glue. "Maybe you should ask Isaac how he sticks the fur on his monsters," she said.

"Are you joking?" I said. "Me ask Isaac Peterman for help? Have you seen his monsters? They're baby-ish and gross. Why would I ask him for help? I'm like a professional."

She shook her head. "But wouldn't it be better if you

and Isaac could be friends and build monsters together? The two of you would be awesome!"

"My monsters are already awesome," I told her. "He's so stuck-up. He thinks he's a master monster-maker. You and I build better monsters in our sleep!"

"I'm good at sketching them out," Annie said. "And you're good at starting them. But look at you, Jamie. Your fingers are still stuck together and your shirt is destroyed. If you and Isaac worked together—"

I crossed my arms in front of my chest. "Not going to happen," I said. "No way. Know what I'd like to do? I'd like to build a really big, totally fierce monster, bring it to Isaac's house—and make it *crush* every one of his babyish monsters!"

Annie laughed again. "You're evil, Jamie. Maybe you'd better stop building monsters. Maybe you should build model planes or cars. Or maybe baby dolls."

She hurried away before I could answer that.

In Mr. Melendez's class on Monday, Isaac Peterman showed off a new monster he had built. He took a long time standing it up on the teacher's desk.

Mr. Melendez leaned back against the chalkboard with his arms crossed and grinned at Isaac as he prepared the model. Melendez thinks Isaac is a star. He's a good teacher, but he doesn't know the first thing about monster models. Trust me.

Isaac is short and round. He has big owl eyes behind his black-framed glasses, and his dark hair looks like a bird's nest that exploded in the wind. I mean, a hairbrush would get lost in it!

"Let me show you kiddos my newest creation," he said to the class. *Kiddos?* I guess the thing I dislike about him most is that he always talks to us as if we're in kindergarten.

The monster was pretty good-looking. It was about two feet tall. A cross between a bear and a human, covered in thick, brown fur.

I sit near the back of the room, so I had to squint. I wondered how Isaac got the fur to stick on so perfectly. It really looked as if it was growing from the creature.

"This is my idea of the Abominable Snowman," Isaac said, patting the model on its head. "You've probably heard of the Abominable Snowman. If you haven't, I'll be glad to tell you about it after class."

Oh, wow.

"I built this with balsa wood and plaster of Paris," Isaac said. "The fur is real squirrel fur that I dyed."

"Genius," Mr. Melendez murmured, shaking his head in awe.

"That's not the genius part," Isaac said. "I'm coming to the genius part." He pulled some little items from a pouch on the desk and held them up. "These are AI memory chips," he said. "You probably don't know what AI stands for. It stands for artificial intelligence."

I glanced at Annie, who sat at the front of the room. She turned around and rolled her eyes at me.

"I built a slot in the back of the monster's head for these chips," Isaac said. He opened the back of the head and slid in the two chips. Then he shut the opening and smoothed the fur with two fingers.

"I can activate the monster and control him with my tablet," Isaac said.

"This I've got to see," Mr. Melendez said, taking a few steps closer to the desk. "Isn't this fascinating, everyone?"

A few kids mumbled yes. I was actually sitting on the edge of my seat. It never occurred to me to put memory chips in a model.

He raised his tablet and began to type on it with two fingers.

A few kids actually screamed as the monster raised both arms in the air.

Isaac typed some more. A low growl burst out from deep inside the monster. More typing. The monster took two stiff steps toward the edge of the desk.

The creature did its deep growl again. And then it spun

in a complete circle. And in a low whisper of a voice came the words, "*Hello, Mr. Melendez. Monsters rule!*"

Kids gasped and laughed and slapped their desktops, and uttered cries of amazement. Annie and I exchanged glances. We both knew that Isaac had pulled off something terrific.

Sure, there are lots of remote-controlled toys that move and talk. But none of us ever built a model from scratch that had artificial intelligence.

Annie and I had never even *thought* of building a monster that could move.

"Wonderful! Wonderful!" Mr. Melendez cheered, clapping his hands. "Isaac, you could win science prizes for this!"

"I hope so!" Isaac exclaimed. His grin was so wide, I thought his head might crack open. He picked up the model and carried it back to his desk.

On the way, he stopped beside me and turned his grin on me. "Hey, Jamie," he whispered. "How are you doing with *your* little kiddie toys?"

Aaaaarrrgggh.

I wanted to strangle him, of course. Instead, I patted his model on the head and muttered, "Nice work."

If only there was a way for Annie and me to prove that we are better monster-makers than Isaac.

The next day, I found the answer on my front porch.

When I got home from school in the afternoon, a big carton was waiting on the front porch. I hoisted it up—it was heavy. I carried it inside and dropped it in the front hall.

Dad came in from the living room. "Hey, Jamie. Hi. What's that?"

I shrugged. "Beats me." I bent down and read the mailing label. The box was addressed to me. "Weird," I said. "I didn't order anything. And it's not my birthday."

Dad helped me tear open the carton. We pulled out the large box inside. It showed a Frankenstein-type monster on the front, and the words: *Ultimate Monster-Maker!*

I grabbed the box and read the front: "Meet BORIS! He's BIG! He's SCARY! Easy to put together. Lifelike—and ready to terrify!"

"Awesome!" I cried. "Perfect! This looks like an amazing monster-building kit!"

"I wonder who sent it to you," Dad said, scratching his head.

I searched the empty carton. There was no card or receipt.

"Maybe Grandpa Harry sent it," Dad said. "He knows how much you like building monsters. You'll have to call him later and thank him."

"Yes. Later," I said. "I want to start building Boris right away."

I texted Annie, and she came running over. I had the box on the worktable in the garage and was removing the packing tape around the edges.

"Boris definitely looks scary," Annie said, gazing at the photo of the Frankenstein-type figure on the front. "He must be big. This box is huge! It's almost as tall as we are!"

"Look what it says on the back," I said, turning the box around. "*He walks and he stalks!*"

"Cool," Annie said. "I'll bet Boris will make Isaac's monsters look like Barbie Dolls."

I lowered the box to its side and pried open the lid. I pulled out a layer of bubble wrap and tossed it aside. Then I peered into the box.

"The head is on top," I said. "It's covered in thick black hair."

I squeezed my hands into the box and tried to pry the head out. "It's in tight. Hold the box down," I told Annie.

She held on to the box, and I slid out the head. Annie and I both gasped as the thick eyelids lifted and two big eyes blinked open. "Whoa. They're wet and shiny—like real eyes!" I exclaimed.

Annie took the head from me. "Ooh. The skin feels like real skin. It's warm, Jamie. How weird is that?"

She shuddered and set the head down on the worktable. "It weighs a ton," she said. "It's totally creepy."

"It will eat Isaac's monsters for *breakfast*!" I said. I dug into the box and pulled out a hairy pink arm. "The skin feels real on the arm, too," I said. I placed the two arms side by side.

I tilted the box and Annie pulled out more pieces—a long body, two legs, and two bare feet covered in black hair. We piled all the pieces on the table.

"Are there instructions?" Annie asked. "How do we put the parts together?"

I reached down to the bottom of the box and pulled up a folded sheet of paper. I unfolded it and raised it to read it. "Yeah. These are the instructions," I told her.

"It looks complicated," she said.

"Not for master builders like us," I replied.

I glanced over the tiny type. "At least it doesn't require any glue," I said.

"Thank goodness!"

"The parts all fit together without glue or screws or anything."

I started to carry the box away. "Oh, wait. There's more down at the bottom," I said. I saw another pile of dark fur and a few pieces of metal. I stuck both hands in and slid out a rectangular gray plastic container.

"Is that the power cord?" Annie asked.

"No." I read the stenciled words on the top: *Brain Unit*. "This monster must have artificial intelligence, too," I told her.

"Awesome! Let's put Boris together, Jamie. Where do we start?"

I squinted at the instruction sheet. "I guess at the top," I said. "The head should slide onto the neck at the top of the body and click tight."

I shoved the arms and legs out of the way, and we propped the body so that it was sitting up on the edge of the worktable. Annie ran her hands up and down the fur-covered neck between the shoulders.

I raised the heavy head in both hands and tried to lower it over the neck. I missed two or three times. The head was so heavy, it was hard to guide it into place. Finally, I managed to slide the head into the neck. It locked with a loud click.

Annie clapped her hands. "Good job!"

We both admired the head sitting on the wide, furry body. The glassy black eyes appeared to stare back at us. The mouth hung open, revealing two rows of jagged teeth.

"What's next? The arms and hands?" Annie asked.

"Let's give them a try." I picked up the left arm. It was heavier than I imagined. And tight muscles bulged beneath the hairy skin.

The arms clicked into place. They stood bent, tensed at the monster's sides, as if ready for a fight. The hands were already attached to the arms.

I handed Annie the instruction sheet. "See what it says to do with the brain unit." While she studied the paper, I locked the thick, heavy legs and feet into place at the bottom of the body.

I stepped back to admire the creature. "Boris—you're looking good!" I exclaimed.

Annie opened the gray plastic box and lifted out a small black disk, a flat circuit board, and a tangle of wires. "These are supposed to go in a compartment on the back of his neck," she said.

I spun Boris around on the worktable and fumbled my hands on the neck till I found the compartment door. The brain plugged in easily. Boris's eyes blinked as I clicked the compartment shut.

"Stand him up," Annie said. "According to the instructions, he's supposed to walk and growl. And it says his cold stare will terrify all who see him."

I grabbed the creature around the middle, slid him off the worktable, and lowered his hairy feet to the garage floor. "Okay, Boris," I said, "it's showtime!"

Was I excited? Twenty guesses!

"Where are the controls?" I asked. Annie still held the instruction sheet in her hands.

Her eyes scanned the page. "Under the left armpit," she said.

I raised his heavy left arm and squinted into the armpit. "Yes. Some black buttons in his skin. And a red button."

"Push the red one," Annie said. "I think that's the power button."

I was so excited, my hand shook as I reached into the armpit and pushed the red button.

Annie and I both gasped and jumped back as a low growl rose up from the monster's belly. "Oh, wow. It's working!" I cried.

The eyes blinked a few times. The big, furry head swung from right to left.

Annie and I stared wide-eyed as Boris lifted his right leg and prepared to take a step. And then we both uttered cries as the monster toppled over and landed hard on his belly with a loud *thud*.

It growled again. Once. Twice. But made no attempt to stand up.

"Wh-what happened?" I stammered.

"Pick him up," Annie said. And as I reached down for the monster, she burst out laughing.

I spun around to face her. "What's so funny?"

Still laughing, she pointed. "Hey, Master Monster-Maker," she said. "One little problem. You put the legs on backward!"

204

I started to say, "No way." But then I felt myself blushing as I saw that Annie was right.

"The knees go on the front, not the back," she said.

She bent down and we both lifted Boris off the garage floor and hoisted him onto the worktable. The legs had clicked tightly into place, and we had to twist and turn them to pull them off. Then it was easy to turn them around and click them back.

We stood Boris back up. I was about to press the power button—when Annie's phone buzzed.

She pulled it out and read the text on the screen. "Oh, wow. I've got to go," she said. "My parents have dinner on the table." She tucked the phone back into her jeans pocket and headed out of the garage.

"Don't make any plans for Saturday," I called after her. "Saturday is Victory Over Isaac Day. I can't wait to take Boris over to his house and show him what a loser he is!"

Annie and I both burst out laughing. It was one of those awesome days.

That night in bed, I couldn't get to sleep. I rolled onto one side, then the other. But my heart was still pattering from the excitement of putting Boris together. And I couldn't stop thinking about how Annie and I were going to show Isaac who was who once and for all.

I stared at the curtains blowing at my open bedroom window. I didn't feel the tiniest bit sleepy.

I sat up, totally alert, when I heard sounds from outside. From the garage?

Yes. Low growls and the heavy scrape of footsteps. I hurried to the window and peered down to the garage.

Moonlight washed down over the backyard, and I could see a shadow moving behind the window of the garage door.

"Boris," I muttered out loud.

Had the monster somehow become activated? Even from my bedroom window, I could see him staggering back and forth.

This can't be happening, I told myself. *The model can't activate itself—CAN it?*

I tugged on jeans and a T-shirt and raced outside to the garage. I shivered in the cool air. The moon hung low in the sky, sending long shadows over the yard.

I grabbed the garage door handle with both hands and shoved the door up.

"Oh—!" I uttered a startled cry. Boris stood right at the doorway. His dark eyes glowed, and an angry growl escaped his open mouth.

Before I could move, the big monster grabbed me with

both hands. He wrapped his arms around me and lifted me off the ground.

"Hey—let *go* of me! Put me down!" I cried.

I twisted and squirmed and struggled to free myself. But he was too strong. His arms were squeezing the breath out of me.

"Owww!" I cried out as he carried me to the worktable and slammed me down. His growls rumbled up from his chest as he forced me into a sitting position with my legs dangling over the side of the table.

"Let goooo!" I wailed. "Let me gooooo!"

Could Mom and Dad hear me from the house? Probably not. They always slept with their window closed.

I stabbed my hand forward and tried to reach under the monster's armpit for the controls. But he dodged to the side. His grip tightened as he pressed me against the back of the worktable with one big hand.

"Boris! Stop! Stop! Power off!" I screamed, my voice high and shrill. "Power off!"

My words did no good. He held me on the table with one hand. And what was he unrolling in the other hand?

Was it fur?

Yes. A roll of thick black fur.

With a loud grunt, he began to wrap it around my waist. I gritted my teeth and tried to pull free with all my strength. But I was helpless against his fierce power.

What is he doing?

My right hand was pinned against the garage wall. But my other hand was free. I curled it into a fist and tried to punch the monster's chest.

I pounded his chest with a hard *thump*. Boris didn't react at all.

My hand fumbled along the top of the worktable. I grabbed at something. A sheet of paper. As he tightened the fur around my legs, I raised the paper to my face.

The instruction sheet. It shook in my hand.

But the words at the bottom became clear to me:

Boris is the Greatest Monster-Maker of all time!

Once you assemble Boris and activate him, he will turn you into a terrifying monster!

Whoa. Wait a minute! Wait!

Why didn't I read the instructions to the bottom of the page? If I had, I would have known the truth!

Boris wasn't a monster. Boris was a MONSTER-MAKER!

Too late. Too late.

I saw the black disk and the circuit board in his hand. And then I felt him pawing at the back of my neck. I knew he was going to implant a monster brain in me.

But what could I do? Now I was too terrified to even scream.

The garage faded. I could feel my body shut down. Everything went black. I floated in silent darkness.

How long was I out? No way to know.

When I blinked open my eyes, red morning sunlight washed into the garage window. It took a while to remember where I was—still sitting on the edge of the worktable.

I shook my head, trying to clear my mind, shake away my dizziness.

I hopped down to the garage floor. The concrete felt cool beneath my feet. I gazed down and stared at my feet—my fur-covered feet with curled talons poking out of the toes.

Oh, wow.

I rubbed the dark fur up and down my body with big hands that felt heavy and strange. I opened my mouth to cry out, but only a hoarse growl escaped my throat.

I staggered to the mirror tilted against the back wall of the garage. I squinted hard, staring at myself. Dark eyes in a bearlike face. Sharp yellow fangs hanging from my open snout.

And it all came back to me in a flash. The horror of last night. The whole nightmare.

Boris the Monster-Maker.

Jamie the Monster.

My huge feet thudded on the ground as I staggered

back into the house. Mom and Dad were still asleep. Should I wake them? How could I tell them what had happened? How could I ever explain?

Hunched outside their bedroom door, I heard a phone ringing. In my room. My phone.

Grunting to myself, I lumbered down the hall and grabbed the phone off my desk. "Helllllllo." The word came out in a deep growl.

"Hey, Jamie," a cheerful voice rang in my ear. "It's me. Isaac. Just wondering if you got the gift I sent you. I got it specially for you. Did you find it? I left it on your front porch. Enjoy! Hahahaha!"

THANK YOU FOR READING THIS FEIWEL & FRIENDS BOOK. THE FRIENDS WHO MADE STINETINGLERS POSSIBLE ARE:

Jean Feiwel, Publisher

Liz Szabla, Associate Publisher

Rich Deas, Senior Creative Director

Holly West, Senior Editor

Anna Roberto, Senior Editor

Kat Brzozowski, Senior Editor

Dawn Ryan, Executive Managing Editor

Kim Waymer, Senior Production Manager

Emily Settle, Associate Editor

Foyinsi Adegbonmire, Associate Editor

Rachel Diebel, Associate Editor

Trisha Previte, Associate Designer

Aurora Parlagreco, Associate Art Director

Ilana Worrell, Senior Production Editor

Follow us on Facebook or visit us online at mackids.com.
Our books are friends for life.